THE ELEMENTS WATER

Poulami Ghosh

PARTRIDGE

A Penguin Random House Company

To order additional copies of this book, contact
Partridge India
000 800 10062 62
www.partridgepublishing.com/india
orders.india@partridgepublishing.com

Also the author of "My Little Trip to Georginia."

ACKNOWLEDGEMENTS

I would, first of all, like to thank my mom, Mrs Keka Ghosh, and my dad, Mr Sujit Ghosh. Then I'd like to thank all my friends at school. And I'd also like to thank my teachers, especially my English teachers, over the years. This book wouldn't be possible without them.

Poulami

Chapter 1

'Um, hello? Sunrise Valley? What *is* that place, an elementary school?' said Mandy when I gave her the news about us moving there.

My dad just got transferred to Sunrise Valley, which is supposed to be somewhere on the border of Nevada. I've never heard of such a place before, but we're moving there. So it must exist, right? And I lack knowledge in geography. To tell the truth, I almost flunked geography in middle school.

Anyways, my dad's job is a killer. We've moved to so many places over the years that I've even lost count of it. My dad breaks down stuff like buildings and builds new, shiny ones (well, at least he makes the designs of those new buildings, anyways). But my question is, why do *we* move with *him*? He hardly even understands the pressure which falls on us kids—you know, new school and stuff. I once tried to tell my dad that I'll be bullied and made fun of, but guess what my dad said? 'So what, honey?' I'm not even kidding. That's what he said.

So this is what I do—whenever we move someplace new, I become everybody's friend. I become the person whom everybody comes and shares their troubles with, and I try to help them by giving them advice, ideas—you name it. That makes me become everybody's friend, which is good since I don't want any enemies.

We moved to New York City two years ago, and now that my dad's job is over here at NYC (he was planning a 100-storey office building there), it is time for us to move again.

'No, it's not an elementary school, Mandy. It's on the border of Nevada,' I said to Mandy while we were having our lunch at the cafeteria.

Our cafeteria isn't much. There are twelve big round colourful tables, and ten students can sit at each. But at our table, only Mandy and I sit because all other people do not like hanging out with the girl who is called the 'free therapist'. Yeah, that'd be me since Mandy is anything *but* a therapist. And I don't think you'd like to sit with a girl like me. I have that effect on people. Whenever they need help, I'm always there for them. But when I need help—let's not talk about that.

On hearing 'Nevada', Mandy's eyes lit up. Then her eyes became dull again, and she said, 'The "howdy" Nevada or the "Las Vegas-y" Nevada?' by which she meant the countryside Nevada or the metropolitan city-ish Nevada.

'That's the weirdest part, Mandy—I don't know.' This was a truth. I *didn't* know, which seemed weird.

'Sunrise Valley,' she snorted, 'doesn't sound so Las Vegas-y to me.' And I had to agree with her on that one.

Mandy is a type of girl who has her way with everything. She can take out your deepest secrets. I don't know how she does it, but she does it. She's the Science Club's treasurer (even though she isn't brilliant), and that is how I came to know her. She's become a really nice friend of mine since she was the first person to talk to me after I entered St John's High (even though all she asked me was which colour of lipstick looked best on her). She's a brunette, with brown eyes. Her family originates from Australia. They moved here when she was only two, so her accent is American. She's really pretty. But she still runs after the cheerleaders, trying to be their friends so that she can become popular in school. She's the only friend in my life that I'll ever remember clearly.

I have two siblings—a seventeen-year-old brother and a two-and-a-half-year-old sister. I'm the middle child, and I'm fifteen.

I have to always go through the middle-child problems, which includes being ignored. My parents always stay busy trying to teach my little sister, Lucy, table manners or searching for a good college to put my brother, Lucas, into. Lucas is what you call 'very popular' in school. You might wonder how he becomes so popular wherever he goes, but let me tell you—it's in his genes. People only behave nicely with me because I'm his little sister, nothing else.

Anyways, that day, on my way out of the school, Miss Rose called me. Miss Rose is the newest teacher in the school, and she is the founder of the Science Club. Believe me, there wasn't any Science Club before Miss Rose came to our school a year ago. She was also my freshman biology teacher, and as I was nice to everyone and people listened to me, she thought I was the perfect target to encourage people to join the club. So she asked me to join the club, and I couldn't say no. But guess what? She didn't need to ask me to join the club to gather members for the club since people just started to pour into the club as soon as it was opened. Well, by 'people', I mean science geeks.

Anyways, she said, 'Oh, Linda, I heard that you're shifting again.'

I smiled encouragingly and said, 'Well, don't worry, Miss Rose, you'll make new friends here. You know Mandy's there too.' This was a lie. Mandy hated Miss Rose. She just joined the Science Club to get to spend more time with me (and talk about the latest ins in fashion), that's all. And yes, Mandy doesn't even know what 'matter' is. You go figure *that* out.

Miss Rose, well, she's a very sensitive person. She's very skinny, and she always wears a floral dress with a light V-necked sweater—even during the summer, and I'm *not* kidding. I think she's thalassaemic or something.

'You're just trying to make me feel better, aren't you, Lin? That's *so* like you,' she said with a dry smile.

I didn't want to make her cry, so I said, 'I'll email you, okay, Miss Rose?'

She smiled and said, 'Thank you so much, Lin.' Looking at her smile made me feel better. In fact, seeing anyone smile makes me feel better. I guess that's in *my* genes.

Miss Rose hugged me, and I hugged her too. Hugging her always seemed to make me feel better too. Maybe because she always smelled like tulips, and I love tulips.

I took the bus that day since it looked like it was going to pour. When I opened our apartment door, I was welcomed with a void atmosphere. My dad was packing up all the family photos into a cardboard box. The shelves were empty. In fact, the whole room was empty, except for the furniture being in there. We never take the furniture with us when we shift. Dad sells them and buys new ones. That seems simpler than hauling away large couches. Plus, we get the latest designs too.

Anyways, on seeing me, Dad went, 'Oh, hey, honey.'

I replied with a 'Hey, Dad' and a half-hearted smile.

But I don't think Dad heard me because he ran into Lucy's room. I guess she was crying. All that I could think then was, *Poor Dad.* Since Dad's last building plan was completed five months ago, he'd been staying at home. And he also had to do the chores, like cleaning, washing, babysitting Lucy, and other stuff. And he hated that. So he'd been online, searching for a new building which he could break down and then build a new one there (or maybe at least plan the building). Mom was at her office, packing up her stuff. She's a lawyer.

I closed the door behind me and went into the kitchen. Lucas was sitting there on the kitchen countertop (since Dad already sold the table) and playing a game on his PSP.

I dropped my bag on the floor and opened the refrigerator (somehow, that wasn't sold yet), but it was empty.

Lucas, without even looking up, said, 'Here, I saved ya some cookies and a Pepsi.' He pointed beside him. Sure enough, there were some cookies and a Pepsi.

Even though I don't know my brother very well, I can say something: he's the best brother ever. We don't fight much, unlike usual brothers and sisters. To tell the truth, we don't see each other around very much. We usually used to sit at the table during breakfast, but he did his homework then (at the last minute, as always) and I read the newspaper. Then lunch was done at school, where we didn't talk much either. And then we used to sit at the table during dinner, when Dad lectured him around and I chatted on with Mandy (using this really cool app on my new mobile that I received on my fourteenth birthday!). But we used to hang out a lot as kids. Those days pass by so fast.

So it was weird talking to my brother. I said, 'Thanks.'

I sat on the kitchen countertop beside him and munched on my cookies. I love cookies. I remember the time when I saw cookies for the first time. I was about a year old at that time. At first I refused to eat them because they had 'black dots' on them (I was referring to the chocolate chips and sometimes raisins). Then my mom started giving me cookies with strawberry cream spread on them (so that I couldn't see the black dots). I loved those times. How come they slip away so fast?

I was thinking all this when Lucas went, to my utter surprise, 'Remember the time when you didn't like cookies?'

Do siblings have this same-thought-at-same-time programming in their brains?

I smiled and said, 'Yeah, I was thinking of that only right now.'

He put down his PSP and said, 'Don't worry, Lin. As far as I know, this is the last time Dad's shifting.'

I knew what he meant. All these years I'd been treated nicely in new schools because of my brother. But now that he was in his senior year and was going to go to college next year, I was scared that I wouldn't be treated so nicely any more.

I said, 'I don't know. I'm not so sure of that.'

He got off the countertop and turned to me and said, 'I'll talk to him if you want me to, okay?'

I smiled to make him feel better. Actually, I wasn't so sure that Dad was going to listen to him.

Then Dad came into the kitchen with Lucy and her vomit on his shirt (for which, eww!). My little sister was crying. I jumped off the countertop and ran to her. I couldn't stand it when she cried. Maybe because I know what it's like crying and nobody coming to make you feel better.

I took her from Dad and put her on the kitchen countertop. Weirdly, Lucy always stopped crying when she was with me. Lucas made faces to make her laugh, so I helped Dad clean up the vomit on his shirt.

Then Mom came back with pizza. She gave one look at my dad's wet shirt and said, 'That's going in the bin. How can you possibly still wear that thing?'

My mom's British, but Dad's American. We kids have picked up both the accents and combined it. So our accent is pretty weird.

My mom kept on screaming at Dad to pull off his shirt and put it in the bin (she was also calling him a 'bloke', which is British for 'moron'), but my dad kept on saying that that was his most favourite shirt (from when did Dad start having favourite clothing?). Just a usual family day.

I started packing up my luggage since we had to be off by noon of the next day. But I received a text from Mandy. This is what she wrote:

Did u knw tht Brangelina is getting married?

I mean, seriously? Can you believe it? And I'm supposed to be her best friend. Well, at least according to her.

And this is how our chat went:

Did u knw tht I'm moving tomorrow?
I knw! I'm gonna miss u sooooo mch!!
Didn't seem like tht 2 me.
I'm sry! It's just . . . I'm trying 2 get my mind off it.

Aww . . .

Look, Mandy, we're gonna chat online, maybe sometimes even video chat.
But I'm gonna miss u . . .
I'm gonna miss u 2!!!!
So, did ya knw tht Brangelina is getting married?

Mandy—she's never going to change.

I'm packing up right now, Mandy. Can I talk 2 ya later?
Okay. Seeya!
Thanks! Bye. Good night!

I packed up my luggage. I was *so* going to miss New York.

Next morning, Mandy came over to bid me goodbye. She was in her tracksuit, which meant that she'd come directly from practice. She's on the track team.

We hugged each other and cried. (And Lucas made an I-wanna-throw-up face. I don't know why, but Lucas and Mandy never got along well.)

Then, well, we boarded our flight to McCarran International Airport, and I bid goodbye to New York forever.

From McCarran International Airport, we were supposed to be taking a car to Sunrise Valley. But I got so jet-lagged that I fell asleep immediately after we set foot on the vehicle. Lucas, Mom, Lucy, and even Dad looked like they were on the verge of falling asleep. But I was too tired to see whether they fell asleep or not.

Chapter 2

WHEN DAD JERKED ME out of my sleep and said, 'This is it, honey, we're home' (this has been his signature opening line for introducing us to a new home), I thought, *Thank God! Now I can finally crash. Biggest room's mine!*

But what I saw in front of me made me go, 'Are you *freaking* kidding me?'

Dad knitted his eyebrows with concern and said, 'What's wrong, honey?'

Lucas woke up, gave one look at the house, and said, 'Holy—'

But my mom pressed her hand on his mouth before he could finish and said, 'That's it. You're doing the dishes for a whole week.' And then Lucas started pleading with her to take back her punishment. I was too shocked, because standing in front of me wasn't a house or even an apartment. It was a barn.

I'm *not* kidding. The barn or house or whatever was brick red in colour. It was made of wood. It had a grey sloping roof with a *chimney*. Can anything be more shocking than this? The place really did look like those barns in the Tom and Jerry shows that Lucy watches. Only it didn't have cows in it. For which, thank God. And it looked really, really old too.

I turned to my dad and said, 'Am I getting Punk'd? Are there hidden cameras round here?' although I hardly doubt that *Punk'd* would've paid for a flight to such a distant place.

My dad said, 'What's wrong?' This time, he looked a little pissed.

'What's wrong? Everything!' I said.

He looked around with a disturbing look on his face and said, 'So I try to bring you out here to a fresher and greener environment, and you don't like it?'

'It's a freaking barn, Dad!' I never actually got on Dad's bad side, but how would you react if you were in my place, may I ask?

My dad's expression turned firm, and he said, 'It's not a barn.'

'Well, it looks like one, anyways.'

'You can stay inside the . . . *barn* or outside it. It's your call.' Saying this, he went inside the house or barn or whatever. Can you believe it? I felt like running in after him and telling him how I feel like about this whole shifting-so-frequently thing. He's my dad! He's supposed to understand stuff like this.

But as usual, I suppressed my anger, picked up my luggage, and went inside after him. Lucas (who, by the way, had already made Mom increase the punishment from one week to three weeks) followed me, miserably.

From inside, it looked like a house. In fact, it was a big and old house, as far as I could guess. My dad was standing in the drawing room. The house was made of wood from outside as well as inside. There was an old fireplace there. The house looked pretty fancy, you know, in an old-fashioned way. There were even stuffed deer and stag heads there, hung up on the wall. That's animal cruelty. But when I stated this to my dad, he said, 'It was a fashion for power in the old days. People loved hunting.'

'And hanging up the stuffed head in their drawing room,' my mom added, eyeing one of those deer heads unwillingly.

I said, 'I'm gonna go find my room now.'

I climbed the stairs. Lucas followed me. We went from room to room. I found this really pretty room with blue wallpaper. Since blue is my favourite colour, I took it right away. Lucas took the room right across mine since it had the secret way out of the house. I didn't know how, but Lucas *always* found a way out of the house. When

I entered his room, I didn't see any secret passage or whatever. But Lucas looked out of the window and said, 'This one's mine.'

I didn't argue since I didn't like purple wallpaper. So I took the one with the blue wallpaper. My room was really nice and comfy. Dad had made a nice selection of beds. Mine was *real* comfy.

I got out of my journey outfit, took a nice hot bath, and just crashed.

Chapter 3

I WOKE UP TO MY phone ringing. I felt so tired even after sleeping for . . . I looked at the clock. It couldn't be possible. It was seven in the evening. I'd slept for five continuous hours, and I was still feeling tired. But then I looked outside and saw that it was not evening. In fact, it was morning. So I'd slept for . . . a lot of hours.

I rubbed the sleep out of my eyes and squinted at the caller ID. It was Mandy. I accepted the call, and this is all that I heard: 'Log into your chat account. Now. Emergency.' After this I heard the beep sound, which meant that the call was disconnected.

I dragged myself off my bed, took out my laptop from my bag, and got into bed again. I logged into my account and was soon asked for a video chat with CattyGal, which was Mandy's chat account.

The first thing that Mandy said to me after the video chat got connected was, 'Why do you look like you've been run over by a truck?'

That was *not* an encouraging thing to say to me. I said, 'It's just jet lag. So what's the emergency?'

She looked like *What?* for a moment, but then she said, 'Oh. My. God. You won't *believe* what happened.'

I yawned. I didn't mean to yawn actually since it's rude to do so when you're talking—or video-chatting—with someone, but, um, hello? I'd gone through enough that day (or the previous day). When I breathed the air in again—man, was I having bad breath.

Anyways, I said, 'Sorry, M. So what happened?'

She looked happy and said, 'I got asked out to Shelly's party today.'

Now I was sleepy no more. 'By who?' I asked.

She looked dreamy, which meant the guy was—'Marc.'

I was happy for her. She'd been drooling over that guy since sixth grade. I smiled and said, 'Finally.'

She looked dreamy again—like she always does when she's thinking of Marc—and said, 'I was just going up to my table in the cafe when he asked. He even sat with me during lunch yesterday.' (Mandy has track practice on Saturday, so she has to go to school and Marc is on the football team.)

I smiled and said, 'I'm so happy for you, M.'

Then she looked around as if peeking into my room and said, 'Wow. *That* is a nice room.' It was, actually. From inside, the house looked like any other swanky house.

I looked around and said, 'You should see the house from outside. It looks like a barn.'

'You're kidding me, aren't you?'

'Nope, I'm not. I'll send ya a pic later.'

Then I grasped something and said, 'Wait. Isn't it, like, twelve or something back there?'

'Nah. It's like eight now,' Mandy replied.

My time-converting sense was not so good, I realized. She said, 'I miss you, Lin.'

'I miss you too, M.'

'So how's your new school?'

'I don't know. I'll be going on Monday, I guess.' That day was a Sunday.

Then Mandy got this message on her phone and got the dreamy expression again. She said, 'It's Marc. I gotta go now, Lin. Take care.'

'Okay, M. Have fun. Bye.'

And we disconnected the chat.

I got refreshed—that is, I brushed, twice (I don't like having bad breath), combed my hair, and got out of my pyjamas.

Then I went downstairs into the kitchen, and what I saw gave me a minor heart attack.

Chapter 4

MY *MOM* WAS *COOKING*. When did she learn how to cook? Plus, our family looked like how just any other normal family would look like on a Sunday morning. Dad was sitting at the very end of the table, reading the newspaper. Lucy was in her special baby seat at the table, and Lucas was playing some kind of game on his PSP.

My mom noticed me first and said, 'Oh, hey, Linda. Good morning.' It's only my mom who ever calls me by my full name. And Grana—my grandmother, that is.

My dad looked up from his paper. He didn't look pissed any more. In fact, he looked happy. Did the bodysnatchers come while I was asleep?

He gestured me to a seat and said, 'Good morning, hun.'

I said, 'Good morning,' and sat down.

Mom was making my favourite breakfast—pancakes with raspberry syrup. I just loved it.

I sat there looking around. Dad had gone back to reading the newspaper.

The kitchen of this house was nice. It was pretty big too. The kitchen countertop was made of wood. In fact, everything—starting from the shutters to the cabinets—looked like they were made of wood. And it looked beautiful too. Mom had got enough time to arrange the utensils and stuff into our new kitchen. There was even a fruit bowl on our table. I'm not even kidding. *We* had a *fruit bowl* on the table.

You know, all these changes, instead of making me feel better, made me feel even worse. I felt like things from now on were going to be like this. Not that I complained. I love pancakes (and raspberry syrup). But all these changes just didn't seem right. It felt like it was the effect of this place. I didn't want things to change.

Dad suddenly said, 'Lucas, Lin, you'll be starting school tomorrow, do you know that?'

'Yeah, Dad,' replied Lucas. I just nodded my head.

'What's the name of the school?' I asked.

'Why, it's named Sunrise Valley High, what else?' he replied. Really, what else did I expect?

'The population here is nearly just a few hundred,' said Mom suddenly.

'You've got to be kidding me, Mom,' Lucas said.

Mom came over to the table with plates of pancakes, and while serving them to us, she said, 'No, honey. Sunrise Valley is a really small place. So much so, it can't even be found on Google Maps.'

I said, 'Wow. So we're here in a barn at a place which is invisible on Google Maps. Just great.'

I got up to leave, but my mom said in her stern voice, 'Linda.'

I said, 'I'm not hungry.' Actually, I wasn't. I was feeling like throwing up. The pancakes didn't seem so inviting anymore.

'You better sit down right now, young lady,' my mom warned. I just looked at her once and went out of the house.

The house looked the same as it had the previous time—you know, like a barn and stuff. I took a picture of it from outside on my iPhone as I'd promised Mandy. Then I looked around.

The surroundings looked like the countryside. It actually felt really pleasant too. I cursed myself for thinking so.

There were a couple of houses a few yards away from ours, made of wood with sloping roofs, but from the gaps between the houses, you could clearly see the golden cornfields. There was a white fence separating the field from the road. Each house had its own green lawn. A few people also had bicycles. A house even had a really old, dusty grey truck.

On my left, I could see that after a couple of houses, there was a sign saying 'Sunrise Valley Market', with an arrow pointed in that direction. I walked that way. The air wasn't so chilly here even though it was nearly November.

I walked for a few yards past dusty red, blue, or green houses. The sun beat down on the road. Our house, in fact, was the biggest one. I looked back once and saw that on the right side of our house, there was nothing but cornfield. And a few low hills in the distance.

I sighed and kept walking towards the market.

It must've been twenty minutes when I saw the big dusty circus-ish gate saying 'Sunrise Valley Market' with a subheading saying 'It'll brighten you up'. I'd been walking past golden cornfields, separated from the road by a dusty old fence, all this time. I came across a few houses and broken-down trucks and other vehicles at intervals.

Everything about this place seemed dusty, as if it had just risen from sleep after a few hundred years and nobody had cared to dust this place.

Anyways, back to the market: it seemed lively and colourful.

When you enter the market, suddenly the dull cornfields seem like they never existed. The marketplace looked like a circus. There was a big Ferris wheel too, with various other small rides.

There were balloon sellers, and there were shops put up where you could shoot stuff and win prizes.

But there was a market too. People were selling vegetables, clothes, accessories, and various other stuff that we usually need. Just there weren't any Target shops nearby or any malls or McDonald's.

But the place was lively, and it made me feel better. Suddenly, I heard someone behind me say, 'Um, excuse me. Please get out of the way. I can't see anything in front of me. Pardon me.'

I turned around and saw that a girl was standing there with a really heavy load. She was carrying vegetables in wooden crates, which covered up her face. And she had two of them. I said, taking one of the boxes, 'Here, let me help you.'

'That's very kind of you,' she replied. When I removed the box, out came the face of a girl, probably my age. She was wearing broad-rimmed black glasses (you know, the ones that you call nerdy glasses), and she had braces. Her face was really sweet, but pimply.

She had dark-brown hair with bangs. Her hair was tied into a ponytail. She was wearing a red T-shirt with blue Bermuda shorts and a pair of purple Converse sneakers. She was even wearing an apron which said 'Roy's Grocery & Vegetable Shop'.

I said, 'That's fine. So where shall I put these?'

She said, 'Oh, I forgot. Please come.'

She walked ahead, and I followed her into an old shop. The name of the shop was painted in blue on the top of the entrance, but as the paint was old, it read 'R Y'S GR C RY & V GETAB E S P'.

The place was not much. It just had this divider table. There was a vegetable centre at one side of the shop and a grocery store on the other. On my way in, I read a sign that said 'New Employee Required. Please talk to Roy (or his brother) for employment'.

The girl asked me to put the crate down on the ground, did so herself, and said, 'Thank you so much again.'

'No probs,' I said.

'So . . . are you new here?' she asked.

'It's evident, isn't it?'

She laughed and said, 'No. It's just that the population at Sunrise is so less that everybody knows everybody. I never saw you here before.'

'Oh, well, yeah, I'm new here.'

She brushed of the dust from her hand and held it out to me and said, 'Hi. I'm Josephine, but you can call me Jose. Nice to meet you.'

I shook her hand and said, 'I'm Linda, from New York, or just about any other state in USA. Nice to meet you too.'

'Why from "just about any other state in USA"?' she asked.

'Long story, but I'll make it short. Dad's got the worst job in the world. Has to move very often. Hauls us along with him. End of story.'

'That might suck for you,' said Jose.

'Tell me about it.'

Just then somebody from behind called, 'Jo, you brought the veggies?'

I turned and saw that a man was calling out. He looked almost in his mid forties, almost as old as my dad. He had matted brown hair with streaks of white. He also had dark blue eyes. He was wearing a black tool belt and had grease marks on his shirt as well as his face.

He looked like he was working on a car or something. And trust me, I'd seen various cars—or trucks—on my way here which needed a serious repair.

Jose called out, 'Yeah, Uncle J. Brought 'em.'

She looked at me and said, 'Be right back,' and lifted a wooden crate and took it over to the cash counter to show the veggies to her uncle. I helped her, without her asking me, since I had this really crazy idea going around in my head. I mean, if I was about to stay at this place, and as Lucas had said, we might not move again from here (well, at least not until I get out of high school), why not try to meet people, socialize, as well as get some cash (and also stay away from home and kill time)?

So I took the other crate over to the table. The man looked at me, then turned to Jose and said, 'Who's this new friend of yours?'

I held out my hand and said, 'Hello, I'm Linda. I just moved here.'

He said, 'I'd shake your hand, but my hands are greasy. Well, it's nice to meet you too, hun. You'll just fit right in here. People here are very friendly. I'm Jake, Jose's uncle.'

'It's nice to meet you, Jake. And I hope I'll fit right in too.'

Then I said, 'So, um, I just saw the employment sign outside, and um, can I get the job?'

He looked at me and said, 'Have you ever worked a part-time job before, hun?'

I said, 'Um, no. But I can if I get the chance to.'

He said, 'Well, it's a lot of pressure here.'

I got a bit of a tensed expression on my face when he and Jose both burst out laughing at the same time. And I realized a funny thing: they seemed like family to me already. And I realized something else too: Dad can move wherever he wants to now. I won't be going with him. This place is awesome.

Jake patted my shoulder and said, 'I'm just messing with ya, kid. You're hired. Your job's from five in the 'noon to seven in the evening on weekdays. Can work extra time on weekends. Will get extra pay for that. Be right on time.'

I smiled and said, 'Thanks, and um, the pay?'

He said, 'Ten bucks per week. Deal?'

I said, 'Deal.'

Chapter 5

It was around nine in the morning when Jose said that she had to go home. We'd been talking all this time. She'd been asking me about New York, and I'd been asking her about Sunrise Valley and, most importantly, about Sunrise Valley High.

She said that she'd heard of high schools in New York, and SVH was totally different from them, and I said that I hoped it was true. Here people were far friendlier than people back in New York.

Then she said that she had to go around nine. I said that I'd see her the next day. She left with her Uncle Paul in his truck. Apparently, the shop was owned by her father, Roy, and not by either of her uncles. She said that her father had left for Ohio a couple of days ago to meet one of his old friends who was seriously sick, so her uncles were looking after the shop. And her uncle Jake was the English teacher at SVH. I asked her if it was weird having an uncle as a teacher, and she said that it kind of was.

Anyways, after she left, I went around the place. I had no wish whatsoever to go back home. At that time, that is.

The market was more like a fair. People were selling stuff; others were buying stuff. Some kids were enjoying the rides, while others were just looking around. But I kept on getting this feeling that somebody was following me. So when this feeling got too strong to ignore any more, I turned around, but no one was there, except for the crowd.

I was just walking past the big Ferris wheel, looking at the children enjoying the ride and some adults throwing up in paper bags, when I saw that shop.

It looked like some antique shop from the outside, if you ask me. The name of the shop could not be read properly due to the paint being old, but I could make out the letters *E*, *M*, and *T*.

The shop looked like a really old one, with torn curtains and scratches on the door and paint peeling off and stuff. It had a glass window too, covered by the torn curtains, but through it, I could see old oil lamps and vases.

I decided to enter the shop. It looked mysterious, which seemed cool. Then.

I knocked on the door and said, 'Hello?' but received no answer. I knocked again, and the same thing happened. I decided to go rogue.

I turned the handle of the door and noticed that it was open. But this place was too small for any thief to exist, so maybe people kept their shop doors always open.

Anyways, I opened the door and again said, 'Hello, anybody here?'

I received no answer.

I entered the shop.

Inside, it looked like a museum. There was a whole bunch of old rocks kept in a trough on a desk. The rocks looked like any other normal rock. But when I came near them, I realized that those rocks were of odd colours. There was one purple rock, and another one was crimson. Others were of various other colours.

I realized something suddenly. I took a crimson rock in my hand and went near an old oil lamp which was burning. I examined it carefully.

It couldn't be. It was ruby.

I again went over to the desk with the trough. But this time, on the bunch of rocks was a necklace. It didn't look like any necklace that I've seen before. And yes, from where had it come? I again got this feeling that somebody was following me. My neck tingled a bit. I turned around again and found no one. I put the crimson rock on the desk and picked up the necklace. It had a black chain wound around what looked like a really nicely shaven piece of blue stone made to take the shape of an inverted triangle. It was almost an inch long from its tip to its base. I suddenly got the urge to try it on. In fact, it seemed like I was being *made* to think.

I thought, what could go wrong? Most probably, the shopkeeper would come and call me a thief. But he or she wasn't here when a customer was looking at stuff. What was I supposed to do then? And I wasn't running away with the necklace or anything. I was just trying it on.

So I put on the necklace. As soon as it rested on my neck, I felt weird. Suddenly, the air around me started churning and turning blue. I could see waves of water in it. Then it started moving so fast that I felt blinded. And suddenly everything blacked out.

Chapter 6

I OPENED MY EYES WITH the sun shining on my face. It was right on top, which meant that it was around noon. I was sitting on a wooden bench which was surrounded by shrubs on three sides. I was sitting upright on the bench, which seemed weird. I looked around and saw that most of the shops were being shut—maybe the people were leaving for lunch or something. I looked around and saw that the big wheel was on my right and the toyshop was on my left. The bench was located right where the antique shop had been.

I looked around and saw that there was no shop. But there had been a shop for sure. Because I was wearing the same blue necklace.

I took it off and put it in my pocket. I decided to return the necklace. Stealing is something that I don't like or appreciate.

I got up from the bench and started searching for the shop, which seemed weird, because the shop was right on the location of the bench on which I found myself sitting. But still I searched for it. Maybe I hadn't noticed the location properly before.

I must've circled the market fully for, like, five times, I guess. The shop was nowhere to be found. It surely had been there. I mean, I had the necklace in my pocket, right? The shop must've been there.

I took out the necklace and kept staring at it for some time. Where was the shop? And was that stone really a ruby? If yes, then where had it come from? And was the shop owner a thief? And was this blue stone some costly stone too? Various questions that I couldn't answer came into my mind.

Suddenly, someone said, 'You should go home now.'

I turned around and saw that it was Jake. He was carrying a cardboard box full of car parts.

I said, 'Oh, yes. I was just about to leave.' He looked at the necklace once and then said, 'Come on, I'll drop you off.'

I couldn't resist. My legs were really aching after circling the market five times. I said, 'Thank you so much.'

Jake also had a truck. It was maroon in colour, with a few patches all over it. He kept the cardboard box in the back of the truck and said, 'Hop in.'

I did so. He hopped in too and said, 'Okay. This place may not have a lotta cops here, but there are sheriffs. So put on your seat belt.'

I did so too.

'Where'd you get that thing?' asked Jake halfway back home. I first went all *What?* but then I realized that he was talking about my necklace.

I didn't answer his question, but instead, I said, 'So, um, have you seen an antique shop here in the market, by any chance?'

First, there came a change on the expression of his face, but then he laughed and said, 'Been around here for so many years, kid. Never heard of or seen any antique shop.'

I sighed and said, 'Oh, okay.'

We kept silent for some time—me especially because I was still trying to process something in my head. Was Jake's laughing artificial? 'Cause it felt so. I also felt like he was trying to hide something from me.

He dropped me off near my house, but before I entered my house, he said, 'Some things may change from now on in your life, Linda. But you're strong enough to bear those changes.'

I turned and said, 'Um, thanks.' Jake left.

What was that? I thought. *Some things may change in my life? My life isn't stagnant. It* always *changes. And yes, I am strong enough to bear those changes. I've always accepted the changes, haven't I?*

But after touching the necklace, I felt funny. *Literally.*

I entered the house. Lucas was sitting on the couch in the drawing room, watching a game of football. Apparently, during the time I was at the market, they'd done a lot of unpacking in the house. My mom's favourite vases and pictures and wall plates were arranged beautifully on the shelves.

I walked over to the couch and slumped on it. Lucas said, 'Where were you, Miss I-Am-a-Hothead?'

This was not something I'd have liked to hear. And I also didn't want to get into a fight with Lucas. So instead, I said, 'Where's Mom and Dad?'

He disgustedly started banging the remote on the couch and said, 'Dad's at work. I mean, he went off to examine the field, ground, whatever he was supposed to be planning a building on.' Lucas smiled since the remote started working again.

Mom came into the room, cleaning one of her wall plates with a piece of cloth. Lucas said, 'And there's Mom.'

My mom placed the wall plate with Elvis's picture on it and turned to me. I knew what I was supposed to do. I started apologizing right away.

My mom only said one thing, 'Your school material just arrived and it's in your room.' Saying this, she turned and went away. I couldn't believe it. She was giving me the silent treatment.

'Did that . . . really . . . what?'

'I know, right?' said Lucas. 'She didn't punish you for going all Hulk on her.'

I looked at him disgustedly.

Chapter 7

SCHOOL MATERIAL INCLUDED A handbook and my schoolbooks, along with a blue cap with 'Sunrise Valley High' written on it. It even had a sun's picture. The sun was smiling.

Anyways, this is what the handbook's cover said: 'Sunrise Valley High', with a subheading reading 'You will shine'.

Inside I saw various pictures of the school. It wasn't that bad, if you ask me (I actually thought that the school would be barn-ish looking). It was a white four-storey building with red borders. The school looked like any other modern New York school. It even had a parking lot.

On the third page, I read that there was a bus supply only for students all around the valley, so I realized that I was also going to go to school as a bus student. And I was pretty sure that Lucas was too since my dad sold Lucas's car after he got into an accident last year in New York, and Dad wasn't going to allow Lucas to drive his car with me in it.

So yup, I was a bus student. What an enchanting thought it was, right? At least twenty crazy teenagers in a yellow bus, going to school. I sighed and arranged my schoolbooks on my shelf.

Then I took a bath and sat on my bed. I Bluetoothed the picture of our house from outside from my phone into my laptop and sent it to Mandy. Then I closed the laptop and lay on my bed.

Surprisingly, I wasn't feeling tired any more. But you know, taking a bath always re-energizes me, so it wasn't a surprise that I was feeling like running a 100-metre marathon. But still, it felt weird.

I started reading a book called *To Kill a Mockingbird*. It was one of my schoolbooks. I don't think that the book was that boring, but I fell asleep. Maybe I was still a bit jet-lagged.

But the weirdest thing was I dreamt of something that gave me the creeps. It seemed kind of animated, but still, I had this nagging feeling that whatever I saw was true.

Anyways, the first thing that I saw was a big round mud ball with a shiny aura all around it. It looked like the mud ball was blocking the light coming from somewhere. Then my view started shifting to the left, revealing the provider of the shiny aura. With a big shock I realized that the aura provider was the sun.

Then the scene changed.

The new scene looked like a temple. It was not an old one. The temple wasn't much, just this grey stone building with four pillars in the front and mosses on the walls.

Then something started appearing on the wall right in front of me. On the wall appeared four geometric-shaped blocks. One was an erect triangle with a line crossing it horizontally. The second was the same triangle in an inverted way. The third was a normal erect triangle, with no lines crossing it. And the fourth was an inverted triangle, so much like my necklace.

Then four things appeared in front of me. I really can't describe it in any other way than 'things' since those were anything *but* human.

One of them was human-shaped, but it looked like it was a female clay model with brown eyes. It was wearing an inverted-triangle-shaped brown necklace with a line crossing it in the middle, horizontally, and I felt like the necklace was supposed to fit in the same-shaped hole in the wall. The next thing was a fire, but more human-shaped, with golden eyes, flaming hair and body (and he looked so much like that fire dude from the movie called *Fantastic Four*), wearing a necklace just like the clay-model dude's, only its was an erect triangle with no line crossing it in the middle and was orange in colour. The third one was really difficult to notice since it was transparent, but if you concentrated for some time, you could notice it clearly too. But it looked more like a man with purple eyes wearing a white tunic and an erect white triangle-shaped necklace with a line crossing it in the middle, horizontally. And the last one was a really beautiful transparent woman with blue eyes; she looked like she was made of crystal-clear water only. And there was something shocking about her too. She was wearing an erect triangle necklace with no line crossing it.

My necklace.

Chapter 8

I WAS SO SHOCKED THAT I found myself gasping in my sleep. The weird thing was, if I was actually having a dream, then I'd have woken up. But no, I wasn't dreaming. *I was there*. I could feel it in my bones.

The four figures then did something weird. They took off their necklaces and put them on the floor. Then something weird happened. In my dream, I turned around and noticed this: the dry, brown surface of the earth was no longer dry or brown. Outside the temple, it was raining, and green grass and plants were popping up from the ground, and heavy wind was blowing. And the surprising thing was, the plants were growing very, very fast. Then suddenly the rain stopped, and the strong winds became light breezes. And the earth and the leaves of the plants dried up very fast.

I heard something behind me and saw that those four figures were gone now, but their necklaces were placed in the holes in the wall.

Then I again felt that blue aura around me—the same one I felt back at the shop.

But this time, instead of passing out, I saw people's faces. First, I saw this picture of a really pretty girl. She had auburn hair and very pretty blue eyes, with a gentle, dimpled smile. Then I saw this picture of a guy with blonde hair and the same pretty blue eyes, with a scar on his cheek. But the weird thing was that both of them were wearing the same blue triangular necklace as mine. Then the pictures started shuffling really, really fast, and I couldn't make out anyone's face properly. Until the last picture of a guy with brown hair and blue eyes, wearing a red T-shirt with a few grease marks on it.

It was Jake. And he too was wearing the same necklace as mine.

Chapter 9

I WOKE UP WITH DROOL on my face. Literally. Now as far as I knew back then, we didn't have a dog. Or a cat.

So I was a bit surprised at first. But then I saw who came into my room. It was Mom.

I sat up on my bed and said, 'Can I have some privacy?'

She said, 'Of course, honey. Well, first, meet this canine.'

I patted the brown German shepherd puppy sitting on my bed and said, 'Where'd you find it?'

She came over and sat on my bed. 'Your father says that he found it on the roadside on his way back.'

'From when did Dad become Dr Dolittle?'

She laughed and took away the little puppy, who was trying really hard to lick my face again. Then she said, 'I need to talk to you, honey.' She let the puppy run away into the hallway.

I knew what was coming up. But before the sermon begins, I like bracing myself for it.

So I washed my face and picked up the comb, but Mom said, 'Come on, Lin. Let me brush your hair.'

It felt weird since my mom had never brushed my hair before. Even when I was in kindergarten, my caretaker—or nannies, as you may call it—used to brush my hair.

I sat on a cardboard box (it was still full of our albums and books and stuff, so it didn't crush under my weight), and my mom started brushing my hair.

We kept quiet for some time, but then Mom said, 'You know, it feels so good, being a mom and all.'

I kept quiet. She continued, 'When Lucas was born, only your dad had a job. I was still in university. I had to take a whole year off before I actually graduated. I thought that being a mom would be a killer. But to my utter delight, your father asked me to marry him.'

I turned around and smiled. She smiled back. Then I again turned back and let her complete braiding my hair. She continued, 'Then after graduation, while I was just about to begin being a professional lawyer, I got another beautiful little lady in my life. That was when life started to feel a little better. But we had to keep you and your brother under caretakers' care since both of us were busy. Your father and I, I mean.' She sighed.

I turned around. She was actually having tears in her eyes. She said, 'We've moved a lot over the years, but I dearly apologize for them.' I wiped the tears off her cheeks, hugged her, and said, 'No, Mom. I'm sorry for behaving so rudely.'

She said, 'I know you're just trying to be Miss Goody Two-Shoes as always, Lin. But we're very sorry for all the trouble that we've caused you and your brother. But we love you very much, with all our heart.'

'We know that, Mom. You guys are great parents. And I understand why we have to move so often. It's because of Dad's job. We understand.'

She pulled away and said, 'Honey, trust me, this is the last time we're moving. It won't happen again.'

I said, 'I hope so.'

Then the cute little puppy came back into my room. It was being chased by Lucas playfully. I brushed the tears off my cheeks and said, 'So what're we naming it?'

My mom said, 'It's a girl.'

I said, 'I know what to name her. I'm gonna name her Tess.'

And Tess barked happily and chased Lucas out of the room.

Chapter 10

S O THE MORNING OF my first day at a new school in an absolutely new place was off to a great start. Mom made pancakes with raspberry syrup that day too. I'd always believed that if I had pancakes and raspberry syrup as my breakfast, nothing could go wrong that day. Boy, was I wrong.

Anyways, so Dad said that he'd drive us to school. No school bus business. Mom hugged us before we hopped in the car. It seemed weird, though. I mean, Mom or Dad was never there on the first day of our new school at a new place. And it felt good too.

Even Lucy kissed me on the cheek. And yeah, I did feed Tess that morning. She was barking happily. It kind of felt like we were off to a long, long journey. I mean, we were just off to a new school, and it was our first day there. We weren't going on an exile, right? So many hugs and kisses were unnecessary.

The new school was good. It actually was kind of far away from our home. It took us almost half an hour to reach it. When Dad dropped us off, he said that we'd have to take the school bus home.

Lucas said that he'd take me up to my locker. He always did that on the first day of our school as a warning to others: *Don't mess with my sis.*

When we walked the hallway, we got so many looks and stares from the students. Don't worry. They weren't looking at me. It was Lucas that they were looking at.

My locker number was 50. Lucas's was 89, so his was far away. Before going off to search for his locker, he said, 'It's gonna be all right, Lin.' I smiled and said, 'Thanks, bro.'

I put in all of my books and copies, and I also pasted my butterfly-shaped mirror on the locker door. It's been a kind of good-luck sign for me all this time.

Then I heard someone behind me. I was never happier to see anybody else before. It was Jose. She was talking to this guy. But when she noticed me, she came over and hugged me and said, 'Oh my god! Here you are!' I laughed and said, 'Yeah, here I am.'

She turned to the guy and said, 'Sam, meet Linda. And Lin, meet Samuel.'

The guy shook my hand, which I'd held out, and said, 'Or Sam.'

Sam's complexion was pale. This proved that he was a computer genius and all that. He was also wearing nerdy glasses and had green eyes. He had a really nice smile, though. And he was brown-haired.

Then the bell rang, and Sam said, 'I got to go now. It was nice meeting you, Linda.' And he went off. Jose turned to me and said, 'So which class did you get?'

I looked into the class timetable that I'd got along with my school materials and said, 'It's English. With Mr J. Russell.'

She looked happy and said, 'Oh, Mr J. Russell is my Uncle Jake. Remember him?'

I said, 'Yeah.' I was actually really happy since I wanted to see Jake more than anything then.

She said, 'Come on. I've got the same class.' And off we went.

Chapter 11

MR JAKE ENTERED THE classroom with a coffee mug in one hand and a few textbooks in the other. He put down the coffee and textbooks on the wooden table and turned around. He looked around the class and said, 'Good morning.'

Everyone wished him back a good morning in a half-sleepy chorus-y tone.

Then pointing at me, he said, 'Let us all welcome Linda Harrison from New York.'

That was when I started feeling a little I-wanna-throw-up-y. I mean, how would you have felt if twenty-five pairs of half-sleepy eyes stared at you at once? I just sat there like a crumpled-up paper, and everyone kept staring at me. Then I realized that I had to *do* something. I smiled and said, 'Hi.' Fortunately, all the twenty-five pairs of half-sleepy eyes were off me before I even noticed.

When the class was over after forty minutes of torture, all the students left the class as fast as they could. Jose also left fast to attend her bio class.

When all the students left the classroom, Mr Jake sat at the table, reading something. I went up to him, and he looked up and said, 'Oh, hello, Linda.'

I didn't know what to say. But I knew he was hiding something from me. But I didn't know how to come clear of it all, so instead I asked, 'I'll see you at the shop?'

He smiled and said, 'Sure.'

And that was it.

The rest of the day wasn't any better or worse. Lucas sat with me during lunch, as he always did on the first day of school. I think that was supposed to be another warning. Or maybe he was just trying to get me to make new friends. His friends were, as usual, 80 per cent girls, who were all trying very, very hard to talk sweetly with me. I didn't eat much during lunch since all they had were hot dogs and hamburgers. I'm not a meat or fish person. But I like eggs. They didn't have anything with eggs except for the mixed salad. The salad tasted good. But it had green vegetables, and I hate green vegetables. You know, cafeterias in schools should prepare stuff like noodles or pasta. I don't know how people can survive with eating killed animals. And Jose and Sam were having their lunch outside the cafeteria—on the staircase, I guess. Jose said that she and Sam had to complete a project and submit it by the next day. I didn't mind much since I don't think they'd have enjoyed sitting with me at a table full of juniors and seniors.

Anyways, so after school was over, Lucas met me as I was going out of school. He told me that one of his (new) friends was giving him a ride home in his car. Lucas wanted me to come along, but I said no. I had to go to work.

I met Jose outside the school. She said that she was looking for me. I asked her how we were supposed to get to work, and she said that Sam was giving us a ride. Apparently, Sam was over sixteen. (Well, he looked older than me, though. I thought nerds always look older than they really are, but Sam being over sixteen was a shocker.) And here, over-sixteen non-alcoholics can actually get a licence. But when Jose pointed at Sam's ride, I understood why people actually let individuals who were under eighteen but over sixteen drive here. Because Sam's ride was another really, really old truck.

On our way to the market, we didn't talk much. Only Jose asked me whether I liked it here or not, and I told her that I did. When Sam dropped us off, before he drove away, he asked Jose something, and Jose nodded. Later I noticed that she was blushing. She saw me staring at her, and she said, 'It's just . . . he . . .'

'Asked you out?' I asked.

'Yeah,' she said, and her blush got multiplied by a hundred. I looked around the place and noticed that it was empty. Most of the shops were closed too. I mean, people don't actually go out shopping when it is a hundred degrees outside, right?

I went inside and saw that Mr Jake was there, out of his school outfit, which included shirts and pants with no grease marks. He was at the counter, fixing what seemed like a part of a car's motor or whatever.

When he saw us coming, he came out from behind the counter and said, 'Oh, there you are.'

Jose went to the sink to wash her hands. I said, 'There isn't anybody outside. I don't think people come shopping around this time.'

'Which is why,' he said, 'I've got you schoolgirl to work for me now. You've got math stuff here.'

'Huh?'

'Counting stuff. There were a lot of sales in the morning, and you will count the amount of sales for each day and write it in the register there.' He pointed at this long copy placed at one end of the counter.

'So that's all I've got to do?' I asked, getting confused.

He started cleaning the car part in his hand and said, 'Oh, it is hard work, counting and all.'

'Haven't you heard of calculators before?' I asked.

He said, 'Yeah. But even someone's needed to input the data in the calculator, you know, kid. So that's your work. If you want any other harder work, then—'

I stopped him before he could complete the sentence and agreed to do the task. Um, ten dollars per week for a work which takes only a couple of minutes? Best. Job. Ever.

Chapter 12

M Y JOB WAS FINISHED within half an hour. Well, I actually finished it within fifteen minutes, but I spent another fifteen minutes to revise the calculation. I mean, maybe the work was easy, but it's always good to be certain.

When I was done, I went up to Jose, who was arranging the new vegetables on the vegetable counter, and said, 'So what am I supposed to do now?'

She said, 'Well, you can do your homework or projects if you want to. Or you can just chat with me. Or maybe you can go help Uncle Jake with his work if you want to.'

I was pretty sure that she wasn't going to chat with me since she seemed kind of distracted, so I decided that I'd help Mr Jake.

I went outside the shop to its left, where there was a garage. Mr Jake was fixing a car. The car looked so old, as if it was a hundred years old. Mr Jake noticed me and said, 'Oh, Linda. Your work's done?'

'Yes, Mr Jake,' I replied.

He laughed and said, 'It seems really weird to be called Mr Jake outside the school.'

I said, 'Oh. Well, then I'll call you just Jake.'

He looked at me and said, 'So where's that necklace you were wearing the other day?'

Something felt cold in my jeans' back pocket. I took out my necklace from there. But I was pretty sure that my necklace wasn't there the whole day. He looked at the necklace and said, 'Oh, there it is.'

Then Jose came in and said that there was someone called Puck on the line for Mr Jake—I mean, Jake—and he excused himself. Jose too went back to the shop since she still had work left to do. I was left back in the garage. I didn't know what to do, so I put on my necklace.

I went around the place. The place wasn't much. There were just old car parts here and there. Dust was accumulating on the top of old cars. There were a few small trucks too.

I hadn't noticed, but I'd almost reached the back door of the garage. It was open.

I'm not usually the curious kind, but I got this welcoming feeling. I felt like something was calling me from the other side of the door.

So I went outside. On the other side of the door was a small pond. There were beautiful trees on the bank. The grass there seemed so fresh, as if it'd just grown. But I got this creepy feeling there. I went to the very edge of the pond. Since evening was almost near, there was a layer of fog over the water. But the layer of fog seemed too thick. I couldn't see anything.

Suddenly, I felt like I heard something. And it came from above the water. Then I looked down at the water and saw that there were ripples in it. I thought maybe it was some fish. But I still got the chills and thought it'd be better if I went into the shop and just did some of the homework that I'd received that day.

So I turned and started walking towards the garage's back door.

But then I heard a screech. And before I could figure out anything, I got this thrust in my back, and I fell down.

Chapter 13

THE FIRST THING THAT I did after I fell down was turn on my back. What I saw above me could not be explained.

There was a green thing floating over me. I can't describe it in any other way. It didn't have any shape, and it kept on shifting. But then a face appeared on the green surface.

The eyes were grass-green. It didn't have a nose. But it did have a mouth. And as if on cue, it bared its fangs at me. Trust me, it looked better without the face, and less scary too.

Then it started taking a shape. Its shape turned into a woman's body, but the body was still green. She was wearing a green dress, which was scratched and torn at the bottom. And she had a pair of wings, which also looked like they'd been torn at the ends. Her head wasn't human. She didn't have ears. She also didn't have any hair, and her head was bald and green with strange carvings and was kind of pointy at the top.

It was still floating above me. I got so scared that I couldn't even get up. Then I realized something: the grass was binding around my wrists and ankles. I did the only thing that I could back then: I screamed.

I tried to uproot the grass, but it seemed impossible to do so. The green lady started coming towards me, and I started screaming even more. Then she landed on the grass and said in a voice which seemed like a thousand snakes were hissing at the same time, 'Where is it?'

I said, 'Where's what? Please let me go!'

She screamed 'Where is it?' again, but this time her face became a thousand times scarier.

'I don't know. Let me go. What have I done to you?' I pleaded. I almost felt like crying. I was *that* scared.

Then she advanced towards me and said, 'There it is. You're wearing it. Give it to me!'

I followed her gaze and realized what she was talking about: she was talking about the necklace. She started coming near me. And I tried my best to uproot the grass, but they were as strong as chains. They cut through my skin. When she was a couple of feet away from me, she stopped in her tracks and tried to proceed, but something was pushing her back. She said in that same dangerous voice, 'Take it off! Give it to me!'

'My hands are chained!' I screamed.

Thank God she was stupid enough to let go of me, and I darted towards the door.

But she was not stupid enough. I was halfway up to the door when another bundle of grass grabbed my leg, and I fell down. I tried in vain to uproot the grass, but I could not.

She walked towards me.

I hadn't noticed this before, but wherever she stepped on the grass, the grass there turned yellow and died. Where'd she buy her shoes from, the acid factory?

She came near me, and I smelled this foul odour, as if her perfume was hydrogen-sulphide-scented.

She bared her fangs at me again and said, 'Take. It. Off!'

I wasn't going to do so. My necklace was the only thing that was keeping me protected. I knew this. I said, 'I won't!'

She said, 'I'd like to kill you so bad. Take it off!'

I just *had* to do something. And don't ask me how it happened, whatever happened next.

Chapter 14

WHEN THE ACID LADY was as near as three feet from me, I felt this tug in my gut.

I looked down at my necklace and saw that it was glowing a beautiful shade of blue. I actually felt like the stone had water in it.

I looked at my feet and saw that the vines which were wrapped around my ankles were now unravelling. But it left red marks around my ankles. I got up on my feet.

The acid lady looked frightened, but she wasn't going to give up. She started floating again.

I didn't know what happened next, but the water in the small pond behind her started rising like a wave. The tug in my gut got stronger and I got this feeling like I was the one making it rise. The water had almost reached the height of ten feet when I heard someone scream my name. I turned and saw that it was Mr Jake—I mean, Jake.

He was holding something that glowed with a blue light, but later I realized that it was his own palm that was glowing. I looked at the acid lady and saw that she was floating no more.

The distraction made me let go of the water, and all of it crashed back into the pond.

Jake said, 'Go away, Ivy!'

Acid Lady, or Ivy, said in a really beautiful voice, 'What? You don't love me any more, Jake?'

Jake said, 'Leave her alone, Ivy. Go away before I destroy you!'

Ivy let out a hysterical a-thousand-snakes-laughing-at-the-same-time-ish laugh and said with that same snake-ish voice, 'We both know that you can't do that. You *won't* do that.'

Jake warned again, 'Go away while you still can, Ivy.'

Ivy looked at him with a really nasty stare and said, 'Or what?'

I looked at Jake, and a bright white light blacked out my vision.

Chapter 15

WHEN I WOKE UP, I found myself lying on my bed.
A thousand questions arose in my head. I removed the blanket and looked at my ankles and wrists. Sure enough, I had those chain marks there.

I got off my bed, feeling miserable. I checked the time. It was almost eight at night.

I dragged myself to the dining room. Mom was working on her laptop, as usual. Lucas was nowhere to be seen, and neither was Dad. Lucy was sitting in her baby seat, playing with her monkey, which made this weird (and annoying) noise when squeezed.

Mom looked up at me and said, 'Oh, there you are, darling. Are you feeling okay now?'

I made a puzzled face and said, 'What?'

She took off her glasses and said, 'When you came in, you said that you weren't feeling well. Are you okay now?'

She came over to me and touched my forehead to see whether I had a fever or not. As busy as my parents are, they never lack in maintaining the good health of their family. They will always look after us kids no matter what.

I didn't know what to say, so I just said, 'I'm fine, Mom.'

Then to change the subject, I said, 'What's for dinner?'
She smiled and said, 'We're going out for dinner tonight.'
I said, 'There're restaurants here?'
She said, 'We'll see.' And that was it.

Chapter 16

Let me tell you how restaurants in tiny countryside-themed valleys with weird green ladies who want to kill you and barn-ish houses look like: they look like small wooden houses with people wearing *cowboy hats* and with *horses* tied in front of them and with dusty trucks parked here and there. But they're very, very cosy.

Here, it was the same. Living in a city such as New York, I've become used to getting ignored so much that I've started ignoring people myself. But this tiny valley is *so* tiny that everybody knows everybody here, which leaves no place for ignoring (except when you're angry at a person). People here think of each other as family and even take care of each other as family.

It's a nice place. Everybody would feel welcome here. I don't get why Sunrise Valley doesn't show up on Google Maps, because it should. In fact, Sunrise Valley should be declared as a different state since people here are so much different than people in, well, for example, New York.

Anyways, so the place was really cosy and nice, and we were welcomed by all. Apparently, this whole eating out to socialize was planned. Whatever. Like I even cared.

Actually, I *did* care. I kept my eyes open all night for Acid Lady, or Ivy, and also for Mr Jake. I had to have a serious talk with both of them. That is, only if Acid Lady didn't plan on killing me first.

So I was distracted. And I also took precaution not to show the grass-chain marks on my ankles and wrists. The last thing I wanted was to add yet another thing on Mom and Dad's list of Things to Worry About Linda Harrison.

And surprisingly, I couldn't find my necklace anywhere.

Since it wasn't *that* cold outside, I wore my pink-and-white floral-print dress that Miss Rose gave me as a parting gift. Along with that, I wore my knee-high brown cowgirl boots, which hid the marks on my ankles. And to hide the marks on my wrists, I wore a white hoody.

And as for my hair, I let it loose just like I always do. My hair isn't *that* long. It reaches my armpit. I have brown hair, like my mom. Lucas, Dad and Lucy have blonde hair. This actually stirs up doubts in people at my new schools when someone asks me who that hot (ew), blonde guy walking me to my locker is and I tell them that he's my brother.

We're actually not that alike. Lucas is always the popular kid, and I'm the so-not-popular kid. He's blonde, and I'm brown-haired. His eyes are brown, like Mom's. In fact, none of my family members have blue eyes, with the possible exception of Gran. But it's weird how blue eyes should skip a generation. Anyways, we're so not alike, me and Lucas. In fact, at first glance you can't even call us siblings. You'd think we're just two kids from two different families.

That said, I'd tell you, my brother is great. I love my brother. He's like the best brother ever. Maybe because he saves up cookies for me instead of eating them himself.

Anyways, so we went into the country restaurant and sat at this square wooden table. A blonde girl with a perfectly happy face came up to the table. She was wearing a full-sleeved white shirt with a pair of jeans. Her hair was tucked into a snapback—well, most of it. And she was wearing an apron which read 'Gilbert's Place'.

She smiled and said, 'Welcome to Gilbert's. I can bet you're new here. What would you like to have?'

She was probably asking this to all of us, but she kept repeatedly glancing at my brother. This was no surprise. My brother has this effect on girls. Somehow, the girls in whichever school we go to can't keep their eyes off him for long. I don't understand why. Maybe because I'm related to him, whereas they are not.

But I'd seen that girl before at school. She was, in all probability, the cheerleader or something.

My brother, on the other hand, grumbled, 'There isn't pizza on the menu.' Then he looked up at the girl and said, 'Why isn't there pizza on the menu?'

The girl shook her head and blinked, as if just coming out of a delusion, and said, 'Um . . . uh, what?'

My brother repeated the question again, this time talking a bit slowly. The girl said, 'Um, that's because, um, we don't, uh, make pizzas.'

'I know that. But why not? Pizzas are delicious.'

'Uh . . . they are delicious. It's just, um, we don't actually, uh, have a cook who can, um, make pizzas.'

My brother frowned. My mother said, 'I'll have noodles. Lucy will share with me.' She looked at my dad, and Dad said, 'I'll have the same thing. Linda?'

'I'll have a veggie burger with French fries.' Then we all looked at Lucas in unison. He looked up from the menu, still frowning, and said, 'I'll have a steak. Thanks.'

Miss Um-and-Uh wrote something in her tiny pad and said, 'I'll be right back with your order.'

Our family isn't into the whole family-chat thing. So Dad, after an awkward minute of silence, pulled out his BlackBerry phone and started working on his latest project. Lucas, as usual, started playing on his PSP. And Mom was busy with her new job application. She'd been trying to become a practising lawyer right here at Sunrise. So she applied at the law firm here.

Well, as small as this place is, it's not a lawyer's paradise, let me tell you. A thief would think thrice before setting his or her hand on anybody's stuff. Here, your family will rat you out if you do any crime. This is actually a good thing. But not for lawyers.

As for Lucy, she was busy gazing at the box-like thing in Mom's hand—that is, Mom's BlackBerry. Lucy was always captivated by shiny things. But she never so much as even reached out to grab one of those things. Maybe she stayed too busy gazing at them. Weird baby stuff.

But the main thing was, I felt lonely. As usual. I sighed.

Then I turned my head and looked out of the window. There were two chairs on each side of the table. I was sitting on the wall side of the table, so I was right next to the window.

I saw that Mr Jake—I mean, Jake, damn it—was doing something beside the pond. The pond was actually blocked out by a wooden cabin, but I knew there was a pond. I could only see half of his body, but I could bet that his arms were spread out in front of him. I just needed to talk to him. He was the only one who could explain whatever happened in his garage's backyard that day.

So I pushed my chair backwards and got up. Lucas saw this and said, 'Where're you going?'

I looked at him and said, 'I'll be right back.'

I got up and left.

I got out through the door and then turned to my left. It wasn't *that* dark, though, since there was a full moon, but it was dark enough to make me hit my foot hard on a rock and almost fall flat on my face. Thank God I have good balance. And also, thank God that I was wearing boots. I passed this huge pile of used tyres, with plants growing even on them. Then I reached the window through which Lucas was looking at me. He made a what-the-heck gesture. I replied with a stay-put-I'll-be-right-back gesture.

I turned right around the cabin, and what I saw gave me the shivers.

Chapter 17

BEFORE I START TELLING you what I saw, I'll let you know that, boy, was I scared.

But it was nothing to be scared of.

Mr Jake—only Jake—was floating. He'd changed his position and he was literally floating. He was dangling almost ten feet in the air. But when I looked below him, I saw that he wasn't floating actually. He was balancing himself on a whirlpool of water. The water was in a hurricane-ish shape, and his feet were just about touching the water. And the water, along with Jake—got it right this time—was fluorescent. Well, Jake himself wasn't fluorescent, but there was a glowing blue aura around him.

I suddenly noticed that something was glowing at the middle of his chest. I squinted at it and saw that it was a necklace. Jake was wearing *my* necklace.

I was so shocked that I could utter only one thing: 'Mr Jake?' (I called him 'Mr' just to be polite).

There wasn't any immediate reaction, but after some time, the water started to glow less and descend into the pond.

There was a really big pond there, surrounded by dense trees on one side and the highway on the other. It was pretty long too since it bent just left of the dense trees and disappeared out of my sight.

I couldn't see things too clearly, but since that guy was floating on fluorescent water, I got a nice look at stuff near me. The place wasn't much, just grass and a couple of wooden cabins on one side and the highway. And there was a dense jungle on the other side. I could say that that place was a major party place since there were beer bottles and cigarette butts and stuff that I don't want to talk about all around.

Anyways, so Mr Jake (I finally decided that I'd call him that) descended to the ground. Actually, the water put him gently over the ground. It bent over the ground like a wave and then swept off from under his feet.

Mr Jake opened his blue eyes—I forgot to mention that he was meditating all this time, floating over the water with his eyes closed—and said with that same old smile of his, 'Hello, Linda. It's a pleasure to see you.'

'What the hell was that?' I demanded. Please excuse my language.

Mr Jake looked confused at first, as if he'd forgotten that he was doing something that no normal human being could do. But then he regained his memory and said, 'Oh, that? That was nothing. Nature knows how much I've missed this,' he said, pointing at the necklace, as if he was talking about his old pal or someone.

'That was . . . that . . . you were . . .' I couldn't complete my sentence. I was *that* shocked.

He just smiled and said, 'Oh, I'll tell you all about that. Just don't worry.'

'"Don't worry"? You were freaking floating over the water. How am I not supposed to worry? Or be shocked? And that thing you did with that freaky, foul-smelling green lady, whose soles are made of acid—well, that's inexplicable.'

He said, 'You need to know.'

'Of course I need to know,' I said in a that's-so-obvious way. But then again, it wasn't that obvious, was it? So I said, 'What am I supposed to know, by the way?'

He smiled and said, taking off the necklace and handing it to me, 'This, here, is the Aqua. It is the source of all water in this world.'

I said, 'Um, can you be more specific?'

'Okay. I will try to. Then let's begin from the fundamentals. When the earth was created millions of years ago, the four elements—water, air, fire and earth—were born. Before their birth, the earth was nothing. The four elements have been the source of creation of all things. The earth that you stand on, the very air that you breathe, the water that you drink, and the heat with which you cook your food or keep yourself warm in winters are all because of them.'

I interrupted him. 'Wait a minute. Were all the elements born in a sort of old temple? Because I had this dream where I saw stuff that I can't explain. You were there too. And you were wearing this necklace.'

He smiled said, 'Yes. So you know about the temple. And also about the necklaces, right?'

I nodded.

He said, 'That's good. Anyways, so the elements had always tried to find a way to stay in this world. Because, can you imagine life without air or water or the other elements? Life would not even exist without them. So the four elements have always tried to find a way to live in this world. This necklace is one of the four necklaces that the first four elements wore. The necklaces were named after them. The first water element was named Aqua. And it was a she.'

'I saw her,' I said. 'In my dream, that is.'

'That's nice. So when the first four elements had done their duties and when life had begun to spring upon this world, they decided something. Can you guess what it was?'

Suddenly, it began to dawn upon me; all that I'd seen started making sense to me. So I spoke. 'They decided to pass on their powers.'

'Exactly. They passed on their powers from time to time. It doesn't depend upon any kind of relation with the previous recipient. It just depends upon the ability to undertake such huge responsibilities. We do not know who the element after the Aqua was. But certainly, there was someone. And the Aqua—that is, the necklace—carries the powers of *the* Aqua, the first water element. You saw her in your dream. All the other necklaces carry the powers of their respective elements. And the Aqua is the one who chooses the person who would be the recipient of such powers. Any person can wear this necklace, but the Aqua will choose its recipient. And each recipient, in his or her lifetime, will have to provide life to the Aqua and also carry on the existence of water. A time comes when the Aqua gets enough energy to search for its new recipient. That's when the previous one loses his or her powers and carries on a normal life. But some powers of the Aqua still remain in him or her, no matter what, to drive away enemies.'

'Like the acid lady, Ivy.'

When I said this, Mr Jake flinched, which led me to guess that he and Acid Lady had a past. I wanted to ask him about it, but he looked sad on the mention of her name. So I let that one pass. To change the subject and also to break the awkward silence that had dawned, I said, 'Um, so you were the previous element?'

This brought him back to his senses, and he said, 'Yes, I was.'

'And you wore my—I mean, this—necklace because . . .' I said, as if asking him to finish the sentence.

'Because when one's already lost the main powers of the element, one needs support to do such an incredible thing as create a whirlpool. So I wore the necklace. Its power—that is, the power that was stored in it by me—gave me that support.'

'Stored in it by *you?*' I asked with a tone of surprise.

He smiled and said, 'Yes, by *me*. Each element—that is, the person the necklace chooses, and in this case, it was me—must store enough power in the necklace, or else life as we know it will end forever.'

This was not something comforting to hear since I was getting certain hints to something that might completely destroy *my* life as *I* know it.

He continued, 'Every element must acquire certain skills so as to use the powers of the necklace and defeat the, er, monsters, who always run after the necklaces. Each monster has a certain amount of energy in it. When an element defeats a monster, that energy is transported into the necklace. Moreover, with every skill you acquire, your power increases, which in turn increases the necklace's power.'

'So you're gonna kill this Acid Lady, and you're necklace's gonna acquire power?' I asked, even though he told me that he was the *previous* element. I asked him this because I so wasn't expecting the following as his reply. In fact, I was *hoping* that this wouldn't be his reply.

'No,' Mr Jake said, 'you are. You are the present element. I'm only your trainer.'

And that's exactly when my life just went right down the drain (which is kind of funny actually since I'm the water element and water goes down the drain).

Chapter 18

I NEVER REALIZED BEFORE HOW bad a timing Lucas has. He had to come right at the moment when I was about to do the most important thing in my life: freak out and scream that whatever on earth Mr Jake said wasn't true. It *couldn't* be true.

I'm just a fifteen-year-old not-so-popular-yet-neither-invisible freshman. I couldn't possibly have the fate of life as we know it in my hands. I mean, that's hysterical. Not in an amusing way, but in a that's-*so*-unbelievable kind of way.

But no. I couldn't freak out. I'd rather strangle myself in front of Lucas, but never ever let him know that I'm a freak who can play with water.

Anyways, so Lucas came running towards us (did I mention that I was about to freak out right then?). He was out of breath. He said, stopping in between words to inhale, 'What're you doing here? Mom and Dad are going crazy looking for you.'

Since I came here, I haven't realized how much time had gone by. Maybe because I was busy getting shocked each time Mr Jake uttered a word.

So Lucas took a long breath in, let a long one out, and then looked at Mr Jake curiously. I said, 'Oh, this is Mr Jake. He's my English teacher.'

Lucas just looked at me and went, 'You came here to meet *him*? Your English teacher?'

'Uh . . . not exactly.' Yes, exactly.

To change the subject, I said, 'Shouldn't we be going? Mom and Dad must be freaking out.' No, *I* was freaking out inside.

Lucas said, 'Yeah, let's go.'

I'd already started towards the restaurant. Lucas looked over his shoulder and said, 'Nice to meet you, Mr Jake.'

Mr Jake replied with a 'You too, Lucas. Good night'.

Yeah, right, like it was going to be a good night for me.

Chapter 19

I COULDN'T SLEEP, OF COURSE. I kept tossing and turning around on my bed. When it was early in the morning, I sat upright for a few minutes. That's when I got this absolutely crazy idea.

I was feeling *so* restless that I went into my bathroom and turned on the tap. I was wearing the necklace. I wanted to assure myself that I really had freakish powers. Plus, I was curious. And I didn't, even for a minute, think that it could go *so* wrong.

Anyways, I turned on the tap and let the water flow for some time. Then I tried to imagine the path of flow of the water changing. I tried to think hard of how the water bent over the ground when Mr Jake stepped off it. And I imagined the same thing happening here.

At first, nothing happened. Then I felt this tug inside me, and the water, instead of flowing down, started bending upwards towards me. The water kept on bending as much as I thought of it. In fact, I felt like I could hold the water in the form of a rope and tug it. Boy, was I wrong.

For some time, I kept on enjoying it all. Then suddenly, the tug that I was feeling inside stopped, and the water stopped bending. In fact, the whole supply of water through the tap stopped.

I sighed and turned around to leave the bathroom. That's exactly when it happened.

Chapter 20

ONE MINUTE I WAS leaving the bathroom, and the next, I was screaming, at the top of my voice, that my room was flooding. Yes, it was *flooding*.

I don't know how, but the taps just broke off—in fact, all of them—and water was gushing out as if a dam had broken down.

I kept on screaming for, like, what seemed like eternity.

The bathroom was already flooded. My beautiful room's carpet was getting all wet, and I was trying, in vain, to stop the water. With my magical powers, that is.

I kept on screaming, 'Mom! Dad! Lucas! Wake up! My room's flooding! Wake up!' followed by a whole lot of cursing.

Finally, when even my room was filled with water up to my ankles, someone opened the door. It was Lucas, who was still rubbing his eyes.

Then he realized that his legs were getting wet. That's when he looked at me and said, 'What the—what did you *do?*'

'I didn't do anything! I *swear!*' God knows I wasn't lying. I really *didn't* do anything. Well, except for bend water with freakish powers.

Lucas ran towards me and helped me in closing the taps. But then he realized there were no taps at all. They'd all broken off. So he just kept blocking the water with his hands. Then he looked at me with wide eyes and said, 'Oh, you're in so much trouble!'

'I know, but help me for now, please!'

'I am!'

That's when Mom and Dad came in. Dad looked at the mess and cursed. Mom kept on staring daggers at him, and he went, 'I didn't do anything wrong. Wouldn't you curse at a time like this?'

Mom rolled her eyes and said, 'Lin, Luke, come out of there.' My mom calls Lucas 'Luke' only when she's tired or frustrated.

Lucas removed his hand off the gush of water through the basin tap, and the water hit me in the face. I blocked out that one too and said, 'But, Mom, my room's flooding up! I can't just leave it like this.' I hadn't realized, but I was already sobbing.

The water had even reached the corridor now, I could see.

But my mom's always been really, really calm in head-banging situations—maybe because she's a lawyer—and said, 'Honey, the water out of our reservoir will run out soon. It's okay. We'll call the plumber right away.'

I couldn't do anything but cry right then. I hadn't cried for such a long time. I just kept sobbing and said, 'I didn't do anything. The taps just burst open.'

Lucas hugged me and kept saying, 'It's okay, Lin. You possibly couldn't break off all the taps.'

We were sitting on a couch in the living room downstairs. I'd just realized that it wasn't only my bathroom's taps that had broken. All the taps of the house had broken off.

Lucas was wrong. It *was* my fault. I was the *biggest* moron in the world. How could I possibly think that I possessed powers to control the water? But I *did* bend the water. That was just before I broke off all the taps of the house. I just kept shivering (since I got wet, and it was kind of cold). And Lucas kept shivering himself, but he still hugged me and kept on soothing me. I felt like a child once more. Even Lucy wasn't as stupid as I was.

How could the Aqua choose me—me, a plumbing destroyer—for such an important task of determining the fate of our future?

Chapter 21

I WAS SUPPOSED TO BE the responsible one. I mean, Lucas is *far* from responsible. And Lucy is, well, she's small. So yes, I was supposed to be the responsible one.

But whatever I did could've been called irresponsible by even Lucas. And you should see Lucas's room.

The question is, how could I be so irresponsible?

So I sat on the couch with a blanket wrapped around my shoulder and water dripping on it from my hair. The place where I'd sat on the couch was wet already. Dad was on his phone, talking to someone about his new plan or whatever. Mom was trying to make Lucy stop crying by going to and fro and making weird faces (which actually led to Lucy crying even harder). Lucas was, as usual, doing what he always does whatever the case may be—that is, playing on his PSP (how'd he get *that* out?). Tess just kept on sleeping beside the couch. I wish I was *that* carefree.

But the worst things were the glances that I was getting from Mom and Dad. I was just sitting on the couch, sobbing silently, like Miss Feeling Guilty.

The water had ultimately stopped after flooding our house for an hour at most. The stairs were all wet, and so were most of the places in our house, except for this tiny portion of the drawing room.

Well, it wasn't a tiny portion since our drawing room's huge, but in comparison to our entire house, it's small.

I'd seen the kitchen—it was overflowing with water. Thank God all the electronic stuff and my books had been taken out and arranged on shelves. Only a few of the cardboard boxes were out, which I hoped contained clothes. Well, the plus side is, they all got a free wash.

Then suddenly, the bell rang. Dad got off his phone and said, 'That must be the plumber,' and rushed out to open the door. And to my utter surprise (and disgust, because he was the one responsible for drilling such a crazy idea into my head—well, not literally, but he was guilty), in came Mr Jake and a couple of people I didn't know. He was wearing a shirt with a brown coat and a pair of khaki trousers, his usual dress as a teacher in our school.

One was a blonde lady wearing a green overall and her hair tucked into a cap. She was also holding a toolbox.

The other two were fat guys wearing the same overalls and caps, and they looked like twins. They both had matted brown hair and flat sideburns. And with those impish smiles and brown eyes, they looked like those two little fat guys in *Alice in Wonderland*, only they weren't bald.

Anyways, Mr Jake shook my dad's hand and said, 'Hello, Mr Harrison. I'm Jake Russell. Here are the plumbers.'

Mr Jake looked like he'd just got up from sleep.

My dad said, looking astonished (since in New York, if we called the plumbers, they replied a week later), 'Oh. Yeah. Um, the incident is kind of bizarre.'

Mr Jake glanced at me and said, 'It isn't *that* shocking.'

'Has this happened before?'

Before Mr Jake could answer, Lucas looked up at him from the couch and said, 'Didn't I see ya with Linda yesterday, outside the eatery?'

My dad looked at me and then Mr Jake and said, 'What?'

I said, 'Mr Jake is my English teacher. I had to ask him about my homework.'

My mom went, looking shocked, 'They give homework here on the first day of school?'

Mr Jake smiled and said, 'Yes. We do. Very tough teachers.'

Lucas just kept staring at Mr Jake with narrowed eyes and said, 'So, like, you're a plumber *and* a teacher?' Mr Jake just smiled and said, 'Yes. And I'm also a mechanic.'

Lucas' eyes widened with appreciation and he smiled and said, 'Cool!'

My dad showed Mr Jake all the places where the taps broke, which was almost everywhere around the house, while I dried myself with a new, dry towel.

It was almost six thirty then. My school started at seven thirty. Mom found me a dry T-shirt and a pair of dry capris, while the plumbers worked around. By the looks on their faces, I could say that the incident had shocked them.

I put on my dry clothes. Mom had found Lucas a dry T-shirt and a pair of track pants. He wore that to school. No breakfast at home for us. Dad didn't drive us to school, and we had to take the bus. I got a seat beside Lucas (which another girl had offered to him).

When I got off at our school, we went to the cafe and asked for something to eat. But extra food meant extra money, so we had to pay for that. After breakfast, Lucas told me that everything would be all right and that I possibly couldn't have broken off all the taps of our house. But I knew the truth. The *real* truth. And it was me who'd broken all the taps. I just knew it.

As I was going to my locker, I saw that Mr Jake was standing there. Uh-oh.

I tried to turn around, but he'd already seen me. He said, 'Linda, I'd like to talk to you.'

And I was like, *Seriously? On top of all that I'd been through in the past twenty-four hours? Now this is* real *torture.*

I tried to stay calm as Mr Jake placed his coffee mug on the table and arranged the papers in his hand. Then he placed them on the table and turned to me.

Before he could even open his mouth, I started blabbering, 'Look, I'm really, really sorry. I know that whatever I'd done was stupid, but I didn't mean to blow off all the taps of our house, you know. I was just—'

But he cut me off, saying, 'The incident is really hilarious, if you ask me.' Saying this, he gave a hearty laugh.

But I was dumbstruck. 'So . . . it's all cool?' I asked.

He got on a straight face and said, 'Of course not! You brought in so much water pressure that all the taps of your house blew off. The incident was stupid, of course, but it also showed something brilliant on your part—curiosity. Curiosity is really important for an element, and not all elements have this quality.'

I got confused. 'So . . . is it all cool or not?'

He said, 'It's all cool. For now. But I must teach you. And I will.'

I blinked. 'I'm sorry?'

He said, 'To use your powers, that is. I will teach you to use your powers.'

Now this sounded ridiculous. 'Look, Mr Jake, I'm really, really grateful that you wanna teach me how to use these, um, freakish powers. But, uh, I was thinking about getting rid of them.'

Now he looked mad. And mad Mr Jake equals to not good.

'Getting rid of them?' he repeated.

'Uh, yeah.' Then I took out Aqua, the necklace, from my pocket and said, giving it to him, 'Here, take it. It's yours anyways.'

'You're not serious, are you?'

'I am. Really. I wanna get rid of them. So have it and free me of them.'

'But that's not possible. Giving me the necklace won't free you of your powers. It's there and will always stay there within you till you feed the Aqua. The Aqua chose you. You must save the water. Or else every living thing will die, including you.'

'Um, first of all, Aqua wouldn't be so stupid as to choose me. Secondly, I think Aqua won't let itself die. It'll choose someone else once it sees that I'm not gonna take those powers. So here, have it.'

He took the necklace and said, 'You've gotta take it Linda. It's you. Once the Aqua chooses someone, it doesn't let go. You'll either save life on earth or let all living things die. It's on you.'

I was kind of tensed inside, but I didn't let it show outside. I just turned around and got ready to leave, when Mr Jake again said, 'And, oh yeah, Acid Lady, I mean, Ivy, won't leave you. She'll keep following you till you kill her. And without this, you can't kill her till you're trained well.'

I turned around looking mad and said, 'Look, man—I mean, sir—once I tell her that I don't have the freaking necklace, she'll let me go. It's on you now. Not me.'

Saying this, I left the room.

But stupid me since I had English class with Mr Jake only right then. The bell rang and people started pouring in as soon as I came out. I said, 'Ugh.'

But Jose came up to me and said, 'Hey, Lin. Where're you going? Come on.'

And I went in. Again. Against my will.

Chapter 22

THE WHOLE DAY WENT real bad. I don't know how, but everybody knew about the whole me-blowing-up-all-the-taps situation.

I mean, seriously, how could they know? And then it hit me during bio when Mrs Bailey was telling us something about the cell—it was Mr Jake who did it. He made the news go viral. I mean, seriously, he's an adult. He's supposed to act mature.

And this was just childish.

As the lunch bell rang, Jose caught me just outside my class. I was heading straight for the staff room because that was where Mr Jake was supposed to be. I was going to punch his face and flatten it out like a pancake. She said, 'Um, Lin, just don't mind, but you should probably not eat in the cafeteria today. Do you mind eating with us, me and Sam, I mean?'

I wasn't going to eat anything at all. I said that to her. Then as she was leaving, I turned around and asked, 'Jose, do you know where I can find Mr Jake?'

She turned around and said, 'Oh, he's probably in the staff room. And if he's not there, then he's probably on the terrace, his favourite place.'

'Thanks,' I said and ran off.

I wanted to try the terrace first because it seemed more not-so-obvious place for a teacher to be during the lunch. Mr Jake was like that. Unpredictable, you may call it.

Anyways, so I ran off to the terrace. SVH was a three-storey building, so I had to climb two floors since I was on the first floor.

As soon as I set foot on the terrace, I just gasped for breath because I ran all the way up without resting. I wasn't much of a running person. Back then, that is.

There wasn't anybody up there. I cursed.

I went near the high parapet and squinted at the environment since it was still in the afternoon and the sun was shining very brightly and the sky was extremely clear.

I could see the extent of the vicinity since I was standing on the third floor. Near and around the school, there was vegetation. Usually I could see healthy green trees. Couldn't see much of them back in New York, only big grey buildings and Macy's and Chanel and McDonald's.

As soon as we go out of the school's big main gate, we were hit by the road. It was this small tributary-like road connecting the highway to the school. That's where we usually drive in from.

Then on the other side of the highway, you could see miles and miles of plains. Some parts of them were green (green vegetables were being cultivated there), and some parts were golden (the cornfields). And eventually, you could come across some water bodies with trees all around them. And at a distance, you could see some shops or roadside eateries. There weren't any houses nearby, which seemed weird. The houses were mostly crowded near the market. That was called the Townside Sunrise (they had this big board up there reading 'Welcome to Townside Sunrise'). And we were a long way from the town side. It took us almost thirty minutes to reach SVH.

Anyways, so I was noticing all these stuff when I saw someone standing in the middle of the school ground. It was Mr Jake.

Chapter 23

Now imagine almost running up to your best friend and then noticing the face of your enemy as soon as he or she turns around. That's how shocked I was when I saw Ivy's face as Mr Jake turned around.

Not that I'm calling Mr Jake my best friend. But Ivy sure was my enemy. And I guess Mr Jake too was my enemy.

So I really was kind of feeling weird when I called out 'Mr Jake?' because the atmosphere around the place was kind of . . . acidy.

But when Ivy turned around, with her evil grass-green eyes staring daggers at me, I ran. Not towards the school, but outside, since the main gate was much closer than the school gate.

I noticed that Ivy's back appearance then was just like Mr Jake's. You know, him wearing his graseless shirt and trousers. And her front was just like herself—evil and nasty and torn.

I ran as if I was running for my life. Wait—I *was* running for my life.

I forgot about where I was going.

Then I stopped dead in my tracks because Ivy appeared right in front of me. I wanted to scream for help. But then I realized something. She set a trap, and I fell for it.

She wanted to bring me away from the school on to the deserted highway so that no one can see how or when she kills me. I just kept gasping and thinking of a thousand things at the same time. I kept on thinking about my family and about how much it'd hurt if I get boiled in acid.

Then I remembered something that Mr Jake said: 'Giving me the necklace won't free you of your powers. It's there and will always stay there within you.'

Okay, so maybe I still had the powers. But what was I supposed to do with them?

Ivy laughed like a thousand snakes laughing at the same time. 'Why so unvoiced?' she mocked.

But I kept thinking. I didn't know how to use my powers at all. Maybe I could've soaked her in water if there were taps around. But we were standing in the middle of the road.

Then I got a crazy idea.

Remember those old Jackie Chan movies where, before jumping up on his enemy, he used to move in a circle around his enemy? We were standing on a road. But beside the road, there was ground. Solid ground which could absorb water and exude it somewhere else where there was ground too.

I started moving in a circle, one step after the other. When Ivy saw me moving, she became conscientious again. She looked at me as if trying to read my mind. I was halfway there when she said, 'Trying something?'

I was *almost* there.

'You are *so* going to be dead.'

One more step.

'I think not,' I said and closed my eyes.

Chapter 24

M Y PLAN WAS TO turn myself into water, get soaked in through the earth, and then get exuded at some other place, away from the acid lady.

And surprisingly, it worked.

After I opened my eyes, I was no more on the highway. I was back at that place where I'd met Mr Jake the previous day, the waterbody by the highway.

The only bad thing was that Acid Lady was still there. And there was Mr Jake too, standing just beside me. I was like, *Oh, thank God! You're here!*

But then he went all, 'That was a nice move for an element, doing that without the necklace. All the best for getting her off your back.' And he took a few steps backwards.

Acid Lady opened her mouth and this green fiery thing came out of it. It was an acid globule. I didn't know what to do, so I rushed towards the pile of tyres that I'd seen the previous day and hid behind it and screamed at Mr Jake, 'What're you doing standing there? Help me! Can't you see that she's trying to kill me?'

Mr Jake said while looking at one of his fingernails, 'She doesn't want to kill me, then why shall I try to kill her? Moreover, my duty is over. I told you before too that I'm not going to help you. You must help yourself.'

The tyres suddenly started melting, and Acid Lady laughed. 'You can't hide much longer.'

'Please help me!' I screamed.

I was distracted, so I didn't see the acid globule come towards me, but I have quick reactions, so I blocked the globule with—'What the—'

There was a huge wall of water from the pond nearby forming in front of me. There were gallons of water there. It was as tall as ten feet, and the water was pretty clear. The acid globule got soaked in it. But since I was not wearing my necklace, I wasn't powerful enough, and the water, all of it, crashed to the ground, soaking me. But Mr Jake somehow didn't get wet.

Acid Lady too got soaked, and she started screaming about how I destroyed her dress (like it wasn't already destroyed). I had no other way to save myself. And I couldn't go on living like this, trying to save myself from a crazy green lady. Plus, controlling so much water at once had also drained my energy. Without the Aqua, I could not fight Acid Lady, or any other monster for that matter. I had to do something to save my life, as well as the lives of all other living things. I had no other option but to do what I did next.

I turned towards Mr Jake and said, 'Fine! Teach me your stupid little tricks to save myself and feed the Aqua! But please save me now.' To give more effect to my words, I crashed to the ground.

Mr Jake said, 'Wear the necklace,' and threw it at me (too much attitude?).

I did so, and immediately I felt energized. Then he said, 'Try to get the water in your control. Don't let go.'

Acid Lady's eyes were suddenly glowing with a bright green tint. I tried to do what Mr Jake asked me to do. I couldn't feel anything at first (maybe because I wasn't trying that hard). But after a few tries, I felt the same tug as I'd felt in the bathroom the previous day. I closed my eyes and again tried to imagine the water bending over the ground. I opened my eyes and looked at Mr Jake. He looked shocked, but he grinned. The water had surely bent over the ground, a ton of it.

I turned towards Acid Lady and said, 'Goodbye.'

I waved my fingers towards Acid Lady, and the water, which had bent over the ground, crashed into her.

Chapter 25

M Y CLOTHES AND HAIR dried off while we were on our way back
to town. And by 'we' I mean me and Mr Jake. Acid Lady had
mysteriously disappeared after getting hit by the water.

It was really hot that day, and I was kind of thankful that I was
wet.

On our way back to town, Mr Jake just kept on laughing. I
don't know why. And I was pissed. A lot. And him laughing all the
way back to town pissed me even more. So when I couldn't stand it
anymore, I said, 'Okay, seriously, what is it?'

He said (still laughing), 'It's just . . . funny how humans come
into submission during need.'

Okay, now that wasn't true. I wasn't submitting into anything. Or
maybe I was. I didn't reply to this comment. He just went on, 'So
every day, you've got to finish your work up at the shop real fast, and
then we'll train.'

I didn't know what to say since I was kind of excited as well as
mad, so I just tried to change the subject by saying, 'Um, what about
Jose?'

'What 'bout her?' he asked.

'What if she sees us training? You know, me controlling water and stuff.' Maybe, after all, there was a way to get out of it. I seriously agreed to train with him just to save my life.

'Oh, she knows all about this,' was Mr Jake's casual reply.

I stopped dead in my tracks and turned to him and said, 'Wait, what? She . . . she knows? About . . . my freakish powers?'

'Please don't call these powers "freakish". And yeah, so? She knows everything about the elements.'

Wait, there was something else. 'You said "elements",' I said.

'Yeah.'

'No. Elements. *S*. Plural. You mean there're more people like me?'

I started walking again. Mr Jake said, 'Of course. The four main elements. There're three others out there somewhere.'

I was surprised, even though it was pretty obvious. 'Do they know? About those powers that they have?'

Mr Jake looked forward and said, 'I hope they do.'

Then I noticed that we were already near our school. And everybody was going home. So school was already over. And Lucas was standing near the gate. As soon as he saw me, he ran up to me. He looked at Mr Jake, then back at me and said, 'Where were you? I've been looking for you.'

Mr Jake excused himself. I turned to Lucas and said, 'Oh, just, you know. Field trip.'

'And you were the only student?'

Oh, boy.

'Uh . . .'

Thank God, right then a blonde girl came and dragged Lucas off. But before he went, he said, 'We'll talk about this later.'

Jose came up to me and said, 'Come on. Off to our job.'

I raised an eyebrow and said, 'You knew about it all?'

'About what?' she asked innocently.

'About my elemental powers.'

She said, 'Of course, duh.'

'And you never thought of telling that to me?'

She looked a little embarrassed and said, 'Oops.'

And I just shook my head in disapproval.

Chapter 26

S O FIRST DAY OF my training went pretty well. Well, as good as it could get, considering the fact that I was totally against this.

I tried to spend as much time as I could in my work—you know, summing up the amount of sales. But how much time could you spend on summation when you are using a calculator? I decided to sum them up using my brain, but I felt dizzy. So I summed up all the amounts once, then again, and again till Mr Jake came in and said, 'You ain't got no way outta this.'

I gave him my I-am-mad-don't-make-me-madder face and said, 'I know that. I was just trying to do my work properly.'

And then we were off to training. Just to assure public safety, Mr Jake decided that he must train me away from the town. A lot away. I mean, seriously, I wasn't Lin-zilla, you know.

So he drove us—me and Jose—up to this field thing. But I knew that this was a special place because as soon as I set foot on the ground, I got hit by this strong feeling, as if the place held a lot of power.

As Mr Jake was unloading the safety gadgets from the truck— which included one fire extinguisher, a fast-aid box, a gunny bag of sand (like, for example, if I killed someone accidentally, we might need the sand to cover the dead body), an extra cell phone, and the like—I turned towards him and said, 'I think I know this place.'

Jose unloaded the fire extinguisher and said, 'You do?'

I ignored her (I was mad at her) and said, 'This is where that temple was, right, Mr Jake?'

Jose said, 'Of course it was. It still is here.'

This caught my ear. I could not ignore this, no matter how mad I was at her. I looked around the place. There was nothing there save for trees and a few highlands in the distance and this bunch of tyres at the very end of the field. There was the highway in between, and on the other side of the highway, the scene was all the same. The grass here looked dead.

I looked at her again and said, 'Where?'

'You can't see it. It's buried under the earth. But you can feel it, can't you?'

I turned around and looked at the pile of tyres and said, 'Yeah. Yeah, I can.'

Mr Jake rubbed his hands and said, 'Let's train.'

Chapter 27

WELL, ACCORDING TO MR Jake, training me included me trying to raise water from this jug and keep it floating in the air for quite some time. At first, after hearing this, I was like, *Seriously, it's like me trying to pronounce 'hi'—it's as easy as that.*

Boy, was I proved wrong.

At first, I raised the water, a litre of it (it's weird how I knew the exact volume of water), and held it in the air. It was really easy at first, but then that tug that I was feeling in the middle of my back got stronger, and I could hold on to the water no more.

I'm very competitive in nature. So when a litre of stupid water defeated me, I wasn't going to give up.

I kept on trying and trying. The sun was almost setting. Mr Jake and Jose were just sitting in the truck, listening to some dude singing a song called 'Achy Breaky Heart'.

I looked at Mr Jake and said, 'Okay, that's it. You're supposed to train me and not just sit there idly while I work my ass off.'

Mr Jake and Jose both grinned.

Then he got off the vehicle and brought me to the middle of the field. He said, 'First, calm your mind. Water, in nature, teaches you to keep on moving and never back down no matter what, calmly. There are going to be obstacles, like boulders in rivers, but water just goes past them, over them, or around them. But it never stops. So let go of all your thoughts and keep calm and just relax.'

As much as I hated him then, his voice was soothing, almost like a therapist. I exhaled and closed my eyes.

He continued, 'Now think of water, water in a stream, going at a steady pace. Imagine your current thoughts just flowing away with it.'

I tried to do that. My shoulders relaxed. I felt like the only thing I could think of was river water, travelling at a steady pace; it was a calm, soothing thought. And then I raised my hands, slowly, and I didn't feel the tug any more. But I knew that the water was rising. I can't actually describe how I knew that. I just felt it. It seemed like I could feel it.

Then I opened my eyes and saw that I was holding up the water. Both Mr Jake and Jose were applauding. I looked at them, and still, the water did not fall off. And then I decided to do something fun. I threw the water, all of it, towards them.

And this time, Mr Jake wasn't ready for that.

The next morning was a really, um, *normal* morning. Mom was busy on her laptop. Dad was busy planning his new building. Lucas was, as usual, doing his homework at the last minute. And Lucy was probably asleep. Well, it was a normal morning for *our* family.

I dragged my chair backwards and poured in my cereal and milk, and I started eating. The only person that greeted me was Tess. She kept bouncing up and down happily. Until I realized this—she was hungry.

'Oh, you poor little thing,' I said, picking her up in my lap. She was a really small dog. We've never had a pet in our life. But I had a goldfish. And I doubt Tess liked fish food. And we were out of ham or any other kind of meat. So I went to the only place on earth where you could know about everything and anything—*Wikipedia*. It said that dogs (domestic) will consume just about anything, *including vegetables*. I decided to give it a try.

Mom had bought some vegetables the previous day. First I cut a few potatoes into thin slices and fried it a bit and gave it to Tess. She sniffed it and looked away. Lucas gave her a piece of bacon (where'd he get *that* from?) and said, 'Dogs don't eat veggies.'

'I can see that, thank you very much. But it's written in *Wiki*—'

'*Wikipedia* is written by nerds who probably don't have dogs.' Saying this, he started patting Tess. Then he shoved the last piece of bread into his mouth and said to me (and um, he didn't actually swallow the bread, so yuck!), 'Come on, let's go. We'll miss the bus.'

I had no wish to walk that far, so I took my sandwich, and off we went to school. No goodbyes or hugs today. Just plain nothing. The usual Harrison family. Only Tess licked my hand. That counts for something, you know.

Chapter 28

THAT SCHOOL DAY WAS the same. No sign of Acid Lady that day, for which, thank God. And the same old training thing. I knew that there wasn't any way out of it (except getting killed, for which, thank you, but no, thank you), so I just went with it. I did whatever I was told to do. I practised trying to control water during a bath.

And surprisingly, I started liking it. I felt just like Mr Jake had said, you know, letting all my emotions flow like the water and letting all bad thoughts dissolve in the water. And sometimes it was fun. Jose was a good friend too, no matter how much I still hated her for not telling me that she knew all about the whole me-being-a-freak thing.

But still, even after a couple of weeks, there wasn't any sign of Acid Lady, which seemed weird. And there was Lucas too, who kept looking at me with narrowed eyes as if I was a criminal, which I guess I sort of was, not telling him the truth and all.

After a couple of weeks, I went into the garage (Mr Jake had decided, after a whole week of me trying to control water, that I was no more code-red-type dangerous, and he'd allowed me to practise controlling water outside in the garden at the back of the garage). Anyways, that day, Mr Jake was, as always, wearing a grease-covered T-shirt.

When he saw me come in, he washed his hands and said, 'I think we've done enough water-controlling practising.'

I picked up a drop of water from the tap (without touching it, of course; I had gotten used to water controlling so much that I could even drink water without touching it, which was a good thing) and kept it afloat at the tip of my index finger and said, 'Yes. Very.'

Mr Jake said, 'Don't become too proud.'

'Look, I'm sorry, but I'm fed up with controlling water every single day.' And then I told him about how I could even drink water without touching it, and he made a sour face, like, *That ain't what I'm teaching ya.*

Anyways, then he said, 'Okay. On to a new thing.'

We went outside, to the mysterious garden behind Mr Jake's garage. Well, at least I was getting paid for this job. Okay, well, not directly, but somehow I was.

I put on my necklace. I couldn't wear it everywhere because I was just tired of having Amber, the blonde girl from the eatery, drooling over it every single day, telling me how pretty it was. Don't be too impressed; she just wanted to get my brother's attention, that's all.

Anyways, Mr Jake said, 'You've done enough water controlling. But today, I'm going to teach ya how to change the state of matter of water.' I just looked blankly at him.

And yes, all that staring wasn't because of the fact that I didn't know what changing the state of matter of water was, because I did. All that staring was because of the fact that it was really impossible to believe that one can do stuff like that. But still, one can't control water, and I can.

Back to the question. On seeing my blank face, Mr Jake started saying, 'Changing the state of matter means—'

'I know what it means!' I snapped back at him. I wasn't *that* poor at science.

'Okay. Well, um, when you control the water, it feels like a flow to you, doesn't it?'

I nodded.

'Now when you change the state of matter to ice, it won't feel like a flow any more.' To demonstrate it, he took some water from the nearby pond. (He still had the ability to control water without the necklace. He said that the previous elements acquire some power to teach the present elements.) And then he clenched his fist. Then he turned towards me and asked me to touch the water—or precisely, the ice. Sure enough, the water was solid and ice cold. The air around the ice was chilly.

I turned towards him and said, 'Now that's cool. How did you *do* that?'

He turned the ice back into water dropped it into the pond (we'd had enough water fights) and said, 'Your turn.'

I got alarmed and said, 'Wait, that's all? I can't do that.'

'You said you couldn't control water, and now you can do that. You can do this too. Water also teaches you possibilities. Water can bend in any direction, flow anywhere. That's how it shows possibilities. Go on, give it a try.'

'Um, okay.'

So I picked up the water from the pond. It'd become too easy for me.

Mr Jake said, 'Now try to bring all the molecules closer to each other. That will make them change their state. Molecules are the—'

'I know what molecules are!' I snapped.

'Okay. Okay,' he said, shielding himself with his palms.

He continued, 'Try to feel each molecule in that amount of water.'

'What, are you crazy? There're like a million of them in there.'

'Yes, but you are the one controlling water. Try, and you'll feel the water and each molecule of it.'

So I tried and tried, but no luck. That day I just kept on trying to feel each molecule. At last I accepted defeat and went home. Mr Jake actually dropped me home.

I wasn't successful in changing the state of water, but it sure did drain all the energy out of me. I was so worn out that on reaching home, I just went up to my room and got into bed. But right then Mandy invited me to chat.

'Ugh.' Saying this, I sat up on my bed and started chatting with her. It went something like this:

CattyGal: Hey there. Wat's up?
Me: Nothing much. Just resting.
CattyGal: Guess where I am now?

Me: Where?

I had no wish to guess. It'd just waste more time.

CattyGal: Somebody invited me to Mellissa's parthay.
Me: Marc???

This got me interested. Mellissa's like the Queen Bee of my school in New York. And she wouldn't want to be caught dead with not-so-popular girls like Mandy and me.

CattyGal: Yupp.
Me: OMG!!! That's GRR-8!!
CattyGal: Ikr!! But I miss u. We could've had so much FUN at this party together.
Me: Yea, right, like she'd have invited me 2. She just invited u cuz u're going out with Marc.
CattyGal: Well, u're my BFF. I could've got you in, easily.

I tried to change the subject.

Me: So, did ya see the pics?
CattyGal: Yea. OMG!! Is that rlly where u r right now?
Me: Yep. That's my new home. Home Sweet Home.
CattyGal: More like Barn Sweet Barn.
Me: LOL!!

Right then Lucas entered the room and said, 'Hey. What's up?'
'I'm just chatting with Mandy,' I replied.
'Oh, cool.' Now something was wrong with him, seriously, because he could've never called Mandy—or even so much as chatting with her—cool.
So I wrote this to Mandy: 'Hey, I'll talk 2 ya l8r. Gtg.'
Then I closed my laptop and said, 'Is everything okay?'
'Yeah, why?' he asked, and clearly, he was just pretending to be surprised.
'You just called chatting with Mandy cool.'
He laughed (it was a fake laugh) and said, 'Oh, my mistake.'

Then he sat on my bed and said, 'Look, you're my little sis, right?'

'So far, yes,' I said, feeling that a weird environment was building up.

'So if anything weird or unusual was going on in your life you'd tell me, right? 'Cause I'm your big bro.'

And right then I felt like my life was *really* over.

He knew about it.

Chapter 29

I MUST GIVE THIS CREDIT to my mom: she has great timing to arrive at my room's door and call me for dinner.

Lucas was interrupted by Mom. Thank God!

All throughout dinner, I tried to avoid eye contact with him. But the bad thing is, I felt guilty. I'd never lied to him. Actually, this was the first time that we were talking so much. So we'd actually never shared many things. But still, I felt guilty.

I mean, if I was given a say-or-die option about who I'd tell first about my whole freakish-water-controlling-power thing, I'd choose Lucas. The reason is that he's the only person that I could trust with that information next to myself.

So I felt guilty.

While going to bed, I took Tess with me. Poor her, she'd been sleeping on the living room carpet the last couple of weeks.

At least, unlike Lucas, she wasn't staring at me like the society stares at the criminal.

Chapter 30

NEXT MORNING, I SKIPPED breakfast, as well as travelling in the school bus, with Lucas.

I'd called Jose early in the morning, and she came over with Sam's car to pick me up. I left Mom a note about this, with the excuse that I had this project to complete (even though our school year just started and projects are usually given in the middle of the school year).

We went straight to school. After that, I sat on the staircase of our school building and kept wondering about stuff that I'd gone through in the past weeks.

I just closed my eyes for a few seconds to take in the beautiful smell of wet earth (the gardener was watering the grass for the upcoming soccer game). When I opened my eyes, I wasn't there any more. At my school, I mean.

I was standing in front of an acknowledged place, the eatery in front of me: it was Gilbert's Place, the biggest roadside eatery in Sunrise.

But the time wasn't the same. In fact, I was in the past. I understood that because of the hairstyles of the people. The guys were wearing Elvis-style hairdos, and the girls were wearing Marilyn Monroe-type hairdos. And the guys were wearing flannel shirts and high-waist trousers. The girls were wearing mostly long dresses or a flannel shirt with a skirt, which usually reached below their knees (won't see them any more now). And there were other stuff that made me feel like I'd arrived in the seventies, like the hand-drawn posters for movies or concerts.

Suddenly, I saw someone arrive in front of me. Then I realized he passed right through me. This meant that I was dreaming (or hallucinating). I tried to pinch myself out of it, but instead I gave myself a nice little cut on my hand.

Suddenly, I froze. The guy I saw standing beside the eatery was someone I knew. He had dark blue eyes and brown hair. It was Mr Jake.

Well, seventies Mr Jake, anyways.

Here he looked just about as old as my brother. He was wearing a cream-coloured flannel shirt and high-waist trousers just like everyone else. In fact, he looked just like everyone else. He looked like he was searching for someone.

Then he suddenly stopped looking here and there and smiled at her.

She was really, really pretty. Her hair was curly and blonde and tucked up into a bun, with a few strands of hair hanging loose in the front. She was wearing a red polka-dot shirt with a long flowing grey skirt, with red heels. She also had this little grey purse in her hand. And let me tell you this, she really stood out from all the other girls. Most of the girls were glaring at her. But her eyes were really fascinating. They were grass-green and really bright. And they were focused on Mr Jake's smiling face.

Mr Jake ran up to her and gave her the flowers that he'd been hiding behind him all this time. They were pink tulips.

'You look beautiful,' he said. They were standing right in front of me, so I could hear them. And I could also hear them because the crowd had reduced.

The girl—lady, precisely—blushed and said, 'Thank you. And so do you. Handsome, I mean. You look really handsome.'

They had this little bit of blushing competition (it was weird to see Mr Jake blush), and then finally, Mr Jake said, 'So shall we go?'

The lady looked up and said, 'Where?' Then she realized where and said, 'Oh. Yes, sure.' They entered the eatery. I decided to follow them.

When I entered Gilbert's, I noticed that it'd changed a lot over the years. In my dream or hallucination or whatever I saw that they had an open kitchen. The place looked even smaller back then, and it was crowded too. Mr Jake and his lady entered the crowd, and they disappeared. I followed them, but then I noticed I could just go through people instead of pushing and shoving.

When I reached the middle of the eatery, I noticed that they even had a jazz band, and people were dancing. And two of those people were Mr Jake and his lady.

Then he twirled her, and she faced me. That's when a chill went down my spine. Those green eyes . . . I've seen them before somewhere.

She was the scary, stinking-of-rotten-egg, green-coloured witch (or maybe the word that rhymes with it) Acid Lady, or Ivy.

Chapter 31

How could he? I ask you. How could he dance with Acid Lady? And like that wasn't enough, he had to *kiss* her after the dance was over. (How did he *do* that? Didn't she smell of rotten eggs?) I wanted to yank him hard, I did.

At the end of the night, Mr Jake left Acid Lady at her door, and like that first kiss wasn't enough to make me want to throw up, they kissed goodbye again.

I kept on shouting at Mr Jake to stop hanging out with her, and at times, I even called him names that he wouldn't appreciate someone calling him, but he couldn't hear me all the same.

Suddenly, the scene of Mr Jake's happy face returning home faded, and I was out of the hallucination—or, precisely, the torture.

I was still sitting on the staircase. The first thing that I did was check the time. I'd been lost in that torture for almost half an hour, which made a precious half an hour of my life lost. Everybody was entering the school then (I'd come to school twenty-five minutes earlier to avoid Lucas), and I did the same. But nobody even noticed me.

And like all that weird stuff wasn't enough for me that morning, the first person that I ran into had to be Lucas. He frowned and said, 'Hey. Whatever happened to you this morning?'

'Uh . . . I left a note, you know. I had a project to complete,' I lied.

'Yeah, I read. So . . . what project?' he asked.

I made something up real fast because I'm used to this.

'We, uh, me—I mean, I had a bio project.'

'So what were you doing outside?' Seriously, have you ever met a nosier brother before?

But then I noticed her. It was Amber, and she was waiting by Lucas's locker, twirling her hair. So he was trying to avoid her by talking to me. I was wrong; he isn't nosy.

'So you're trying to get Blondie there off your back?' I asked, lifting an eyebrow.

'Smile. Keep smiling and talking to me. Yes,' he answered, trying to smile himself even though his back was turned to Amber.

I smiled and said, 'How may I help you?'

He looked relieved and said, 'Uh, just tell her that you need to talk to the principal with me.'

'To complain about you?' I asked. Why would a guy want his sister to say something like that?

Then he started saying, 'No! Not complain. Just talk, maybe, about our, um, family stuff.'

'Why would we wanna feed the principal stuff abo—'

'Just help me, will you!' he said, getting restless.

I chuckled and said, 'Okay. Calm down! Just tell me this: why can't *you* tell that to her?'

'Because I've tried that a thousand times, and it just got old. This time, she won't believe me. She's gonna stick with me until I enter the principal's room.'

'And how do you know that she's not gonna do the same if I tell her that we need to talk to the principal, huh? I don't wanna get into any trouble.'

'You won't. Just help me get her off my back.'

I rolled my eyes and said, 'Okay.'

Then I went over to Amber while dragging Lucas along with me and said, 'Amber, I'm so sorry. I just need to borrow my brother for a couple o' minutes.'

She smiled and said, 'Okey-dokey! Just call me later, Luke!'

Nobody calls Lucas 'Luke' except for Mom and sometimes even me. This Amber girl was a real pain.

As soon as we were out of Amber's sight, Lucas let out a long sigh and said, 'Thanks. I owe you. Big time.'

'That's okay. It's just, if you don't like her, why lead her on?' I asked.

'I am not leading her on. We didn't even go out, except in her imaginary Amber world. She's just so clingy to me all the time. It's frustrating!'

'Well, you better watch out for yourself, buddy,' I said. Then I started walking back to my locker.

Lucas grabbed my arm and said, 'Don't go there now.'

'What! But I gotta grab my books!'

'Not now!'

'Now, Lucas! I have class!'

He shoved me into the chem. lab and entered it too. He kept on looking through the small glass piece in the door. Then after a minute, he exhaled and opened the door and said, 'Now you can go.'

What a baby.

I rolled my eyes again and went to my locker.

I grabbed my books and went off to class.

Chapter 32

As I HOPPED INTO Sam's car (he dropped us at the shop every day), I asked Jose, 'Whatever happened to Mr Jake? Didn't see him in English today.'

She said, 'He had work,' which was the code word for trouble.

'Oh,' I replied. This wasn't any code word.

As soon as Sam left, I turned to Jose and said, 'What happened?'

She said, 'Come on in.'

As soon as I entered the garage, I said, 'Holy—'

Because the garage was destroyed. Absolutely destroyed. The cars and the car parts were burnt. The back wall of the garage seemed like it'd melted. We could clearly see the green trees at the back of the garage. But the trees were half burnt. And by burnt, I don't mean burnt with fire, but with acid.

And the owner of this garage kissed the destroyer of his garage. Huh.

Mr Jake was standing there in the middle of the mess. He was holding what seemed like half a steering wheel. Some of the cars only had the melted tyres left.

'Acid Lady happened,' said Jose.

I made my way through the mess and, standing near Mr Jake, said, 'When did this happen?'

'Last night. This morning. I don't know exactly,' he replied.

'Huh. And the culprit is the girl you kissed.' And as soon as I said it, I regretted it. He turned to look at me. Then he said, 'Jose, honey, would you bring me the phone and the notebook beside it?'

Jose looked happy to leave. Then he turned towards me and said, 'What did you say just now?'

'Uh, it's just I had this vision thingy this morning. I saw Acid Lady and you dancing at Gilbert's Place and, um . . . kissing,' I said, not being able to look him in the eyes.

'Her name's Ivy. And that's none of your business, so stay out of it. Just learn whatever I'm teaching you.'

That's when I got mad. I had a right to know whatever happened between them if I was to kill her eventually. But I suppressed the anger and said, 'I'm sorry. I can't help my hallucinations.'

Just then Jose arrived (I was actually praying madly for her to arrive), and that was it about our whole discussion on the Ivy-Mr Jake relation.

After we cleaned up the garage (which meant throwing out everything that was burnt), Jose said that Sam was supposed to come over with his truck since they had a date, so they could drop me off. I said that I didn't want to destroy their date, and she said, 'Oh, you ain't gonna destroy it. Your house is along the way to the theatre.'

I got surprised and said, 'There's a movie theatre here?'

She laughed and said, dusting her hands, 'Sunrise Valley isn't *that* unattached to the world, you know.'

I laughed and said, 'Yeah, I know. It was just . . . kinda surprising.'

Then Mr Jake came in and said, 'The truck drove away the burnt stuff to the dump. I just gotta take care of some financial stuff now.'

'Is everything okay with finances? Was much damage caused?' Jose asked.

He looked around the garage and said, 'No. Not much damage caused.' Then he laughed and, giving Jose a pat on the back, said, 'You needn't worry, dear. It'll be fine.'

'I can stay and help you with the rest of the clean-up if you want,' Jose said even though she didn't want to miss her date.

'No, honey, it's fine. Just have fun on your date.' Saying this, Mr Jake went back to the shop.

I went over to Jose and said, 'He'll be okay?'

She nodded, even if she wasn't so sure, and said, 'He'll be okay.'

Then we heard Sam's truck. As he got out, he said, 'Did you guys figure out who did this?' I looked at Jose, and she looked back at me. Then she looked back at Sam and said, 'Oh, it was probably some chemical reaction between the materials with which the garage was made and the . . . um, new paint.'

Sam didn't look that assured, but he said, 'Oookay, and what about the car parts?'

Jose looked at me, like, *A little help here, please?*

And I said, 'The same paint was used on the car parts.'

Jose looked at me like, *Seriously?*

Sam said, 'Why would you guys paint the car parts?'

I said, 'I'm sorry, but I'm gonna be late. I was supposed to go home early today. So shall we go?'

Sam looked at me and said, 'Uh . . . sure.' Then he looked at Jose and said, 'You ready to go?'

Jose nodded. But she was staring daggers at me all the way home because I got myself out of it, somehow, and she was still stuck with Sam, and Sam wasn't going to let it go that fast.

Before I got off, I mouthed *sorry* to Jose, and she replied back with something not nice.

I went to the kitchen directly. Mom was cooking as well as working on her laptop, and she was also taking care of Lucy. My multitasking Mom.

'Hey, Mom,' I said, keeping my bag on the table.

She looked up from her laptop just to say, 'Hey, honey.'

'So . . . what're you doing?'

I looked into the laptop screen and saw that she was writing something. She said, 'Oh, I'm working as an online lawyer for this guy in New Orleans.'

I looked at her and said, 'You can *do* that?'

'I guess.'

I went out to the living room, but Lucas was there. As I was avoiding him, I went to Dad's working room instead.

He was still drawing stupid building stuff. I never got how people actually build stuff that Dad draws. I went over to the empty chair beside him. He was drawing on a graph kept on the famous sloping table, with a lamp aimed directly on the paper. On seeing me, he said, 'Hey there, honey.'

'Hey, Dad. What're you doing?'

'Working. Where've you been all this time? It's almost'—he looked at his watch and continued—'seven.'

'Took you guys long enough to figure *that* out. I just got this job at a shop. It's my friend's father's shop. She works there too.' I was glad that at least someone in my family noticed my absence.

'So my baby girl's growing up?' he asked, looking at me.

'Your "baby girl's" been growing up since a long time. You just noticed it now.'

He stopped drawing abruptly and faced me. 'I'm sorry, honey, that I've been busy.' He actually looked sorry.

'It's okay, Dad.' I got up and said, 'So I'll just leave you to your work now, I guess.'

Just then his phone rang, and I said, 'There you go.'

And I went back to my room. I practised trying to change the state of water while taking a shower. No such luck. Then I did my homework.

Nothing awkward or special happened that night. We had our dinner together, but it was just like the old times. Mom worked at the table, Dad talked with this dude on his phone all throughout dinner. Lucas kept playing on his PSP as well as eating. Lucy did baby stuff. And as for me, I ate my dinner and went back to sleep. No dreams or nightmares. Just sound sleep.

And it was all awkward from my point of view.

Chapter 33

IT'S BEEN TWO WEEKS since the destruction of the garage. Jose's dad, Mr Roy, came back from his visit, and he obviously wasn't happy about it all. It seemed like he didn't know anything about Acid Lady or the elements.

I'd succeeded in changing the state of water, but I couldn't keep it in that state for a long time. I'd been practising that too. My necklace has started shining a bit. Mr Jake said that the more tricks I could learn, the more power is stored into the necklace. And if I succeed in killing Acid Lady, then I'd get bonus powers. It's like a big real-life video game, if you ask me.

Lucas was still sometimes using me to get away from Amber. But he'd finally decided to give it a try. Dating Amber, I mean.

Everything was going great, which was weird. Acid Lady didn't show up after her big break-in. Mr Jake said that maybe she was eating acid to increase her powers, and I kept wondering whether she could really do that.

But I had this dream one night which changed it all.

What I saw at first was a guy's face. He was handsome. He had blue eyes like mine and dark brown hair. And he had this really cute smile to die for.

At first the dream was focusing only on his face, but later it zoomed out, and I saw what he was wearing on his neck: it was Aqua. At first I thought that maybe he was the element before Mr Jake.

But then the scene changed, and I saw Mr Jake standing by the pond behind Gilbert's Place. And his hands were spread, palms out, in front of him, and I saw that the water was churning. Slowly, it started to form a small water hurricane. Mr Jake had taught me this while I was still stuck with controlling water.

Then he turned to his left, and so did my vision. I saw the guy that I'd seen before standing there. He was probably as old as me. He said, 'Cool.'

'Now you give it a try,' said Mr Jake. He let go of the water that he was controlling. The guy was still wearing Aqua.

But when Mr Jake asked him to give it a try, it felt like the cute guy was his student, not the other way. Then why did Mr Jake say that he was the element before me?

The guy did it pretty swiftly, I have to say, better than me, even, when I tried it for the first time.

Then the scene dissolved and left me to wonder whatever had happened.

Who was the guy? And why was Mr Jake teaching him elemental skills? I was the immediate element after Mr Jake. He himself said that. Then who was the guy?

Suddenly, something appeared in my view. I saw the cute guy, and then I saw Acid Lady. They were standing side by side.

In the background I saw a big waterbody surrounded by trees. And in the distance, all I could see was golden plains as far as my vision would go. There was a young green tree beside the pond and a few green hedges, some dry ones too. I thought that I'd seen that place before.

And if you ask me, the cute guy didn't look cute any more. In fact, he looked evil. And his blue eyes had turned green, the same colour as Acid Lady's.

The scene zoomed out, and I saw that I was standing beside Mr Jake. His face looked dirty, as if he'd been working at the garage non-stop.

He said, 'Let him go, Ivy.' He didn't look at her with affection any more.

Acid Lady's face suddenly started changing, and she looked like the girl that Mr Jake kissed. And the worst thing was, they were both the same person.

Anyways, Acid Lady turned into Ivy and said in Ivy's voice, 'You do love me, Jake, don't you? Then how can you hurt me?'

Then her face changed back to that alien-ish creature, and she gave out a laugh.

I looked at Mr Jake and wondered why he wasn't killing her. But what I saw surprised me. Mr Jake was crying. He was literally in tears. His expression didn't change. He looked at the ground, and I saw that there was a fallen diamond ring there.

He picked it up and looked at Acid Lady and said, 'I bought this for you because I loved you. Don't make me do this. Let the boy go.'

And like it always happens, my dream ended. It wouldn't have ended if it wasn't for Tess jumping up on my bed and licking my face. I got her off my bed and said, 'Bad Tess. You didn't let me complete my dream!' She turned and left the room.

Then I tried to go back to sleep, but I didn't get the same dream. So I got up, brushed my teeth, bathed, combed my hair, and went downstairs into the kitchen.

But guess what I saw? An empty kitchen. I looked at the clock and saw that it was almost nine in the morning, but still my parents weren't awake.

Then I remembered what day it was: it was Saturday.

I poured my cornflakes into cold milk, had it, and left the house.

This time, I didn't write any note.

I walked all the way to Roy's place. Since Mr Roy came back, he'd been staying at the counter. Mr Jake spent most of his time at the garage, looking over the workers who repaired the garage. And when the time came to train me, he left his duty to Jose, and we went to that place again where the temple was situated.

It was a long walk, and I jogged more than walked. When I reached the market, I saw that it was crowded. Apparently, people didn't sleep like sloths here on weekends, unlike my family.

When I entered the shop, Mr Roy greeted me a good morning, and so did Jose. I didn't do my summing-up work first. I asked Jose where Mr Jake was. She told me that he was at the garage.

I entered the garage and saw that the repair work was done. 'Wow,' I said, 'they did a good job.'

'It'll never be like before,' said Mr Jake, without even looking up from the car which he was repairing. He looked mad about something.

'So . . . I wanted to ask you something,' I asked with precaution.

He looked up at me and said, 'Does this involve my and Ivy's past?'

'Kinda,' I replied.

'I'm busy.'

'Look, if I'm gonna kill her, I better know why I'm doing that.'

'She tried to kill you. Any other reason you want?'

'Am I the immediate element after you? Or was there somebody else? A guy?'

This caught his ear. 'You saw him?' he asked.

'Yes, in my dream. Please don't keep secrets. I don't like secrets.'

He looked serious and said, 'Nobody likes secrets.'

Then he washed his hands at the basin and sat on a metal box. He gestured at me to sit on the half car in front of him.

'To answer your question, no, you aren't the immediate element after me. And yes, there was a guy,' he began.

'What happened to him?'

'Acid Lady happened to him.'

'Translation, please?'

'He fell into the clutches of Acid Lady. She lured him into accepting her reward, which always ends in death.'

I kept quiet. Mr Jake looked out of the front door of the garage and said, 'When a new element is born, the previous one gets signs from the Aqua. You just . . . get to know that a new one is born. When I got the signal, I was extremely happy because I had a girl that I wanted to make my wife. I was just waiting for the new element to be born so that I could give up this hazardous life and live like a normal guy again. Not that I didn't like the powers—I loved them, but still.' He sighed.

'Tell me about it,' I added, rolling my eyes.

He laughed quietly and continued, 'The new element was the guy you saw in your dream. And luckily, he was born in Sunrise Valley only. I started training him. My relationship with Ivy—I still didn't know her dual personality—was going great. In fact, I'd even bought a diamond ring for her. But then, slowly, I realized that Mike—that was the new element's name—was becoming worse day by day. He wasn't paying proper attention either. Then one day, I noticed his eyes. They weren't blue any more—and all water elements have blue eyes. His eyes had turned green. That's when I realized something was wrong.'

I think I must mention this: his eyes had watered up.

He continued, 'Then one day, I called him to have a talk with him. I realized that he was under the influence of a new monster.'

I murmured, 'Monster it is.'

He glared at me and continued, 'So I realized that he was under the influence of *something unusual*. When I called him that day, Ivy came with him. But then she changed form in front of me, and she turned into that hideous creature.'

A tear rolled down his cheek.

'The diamond ring fell from my hand. It was in my hand because I was just looking at it. I tried to bring Mike back, but he was already too deep under the influence, too gone.' He stopped.

'What happened then?' I urged on.

'I killed him.' Saying this, he dusted his hands and got up.

'Whoa, whoa, wait. What?'

He looked at me and said, 'I had no other choice but to kill him. Yes, I killed an element. But I did that to save the next element—that is you—a lot of trouble. If I didn't kill him, then there would've been another monster for you to kill. And maybe he'd have killed you even before you learned the skills. Ivy fled from me. I was trying to kill her, hoping that as soon as she dies, the influence over Mike will end, but I killed Mike instead. So yes, I'm a killer.'

'You're not a killer, Mr Jake,' I said. 'You were just trying to protect us.'

'That, and I'm also a killer.'

'Then what happened?'

'That was it. Aqua said that by the time Mike was killed, a new element—you—were already born. She also restored certain powers of mine until you were old enough. So I just had to wait, uh, fifteen more years. And the earth finally wasn't destroyed because of me. That's all.'

And he started working again, and I realized he didn't want to talk about it any more (and if I did ask him about it, I'd just make things worse).

So I left and went into the shop to do my job.

Chapter 34

S INCE I GOT TO know about the whole Mike thing, I couldn't concentrate on whatever I was doing.

I did my job at the shop, and after two hours, I went back to the garage to check on Mr Jake. But I didn't find him there.

I asked Jose whether she knew where Mr Jake was, but she said she didn't know that. She also told me that Mr Jake should be left alone for some time to figure stuff out.

But I knew that that was not to be.

So I borrowed Sam's car (he'd been hanging around the shop since he started dating Jose) and drove it up to the temple place.

Yes, I knew how to drive a car. I used to play this game where you had to drive a car, and it just felt real. Moreover, once or twice, I drove my brother's car back in New York. There weren't any sheriffs around, so I got a pass.

When I reached the temple place, I saw that Mr Jake was sitting on the fence surrounding the field, staring at nothing.

I stopped the car a few feet ahead of his view and got out of it. He didn't look at me. I went over and sat beside him and kept silent. I decided it'd be best for him to start the conversation.

After a few minutes he pointed at a tree beside the pond on the other side of the road. The tree was dead. In fact, the surrounding area looked dead too.

He said, 'See that tree?'

'Yeah. What about it?' I asked.

'That's where I killed Mike. I was aiming at Ivy, but Ivy fled, leaving him to his fate.' Then he paused.

I kept silent.

'Do you know what Mike did just before he got under Ivy's influence?' he asked, looking at me.

I shook my head.

'He tried to give up his powers, just like you did. He gave Aqua back to me. That's why he went under Ivy's influence. I could've saved him, but I was too busy planning to propose to the woman I thought was the love of my life. Moreover, I didn't know that something *that* bad could happen. I was new at this thing, you know.'

There was a long silence.

'So, like, Aqua also saves us from the influence of bad monsters?' I asked.

He nodded.

I looked at him and said, 'I'm glad that Aqua chose me for such a huge task. And I'm happy that I didn't quit permanently.'

He smiled and looked back at the tree.

I decided that it was probably the best time for some good news.

So I waved my hand upwards in front of me, and some of the water rose from the nearby waterbody. Then I dragged the water towards us.

He asked, 'What're you doing?'

Instead of replying, I closed my fist, freezing the water, and looked at him with a grin.

'Nice, but how long can you hold it?' he said, grinning.

'As long as you want,' I replied.

'You can't do that,' he said.

I frowned and said, 'Why not?'

He got off the fence and, dusting his hands, said, 'Because ice will melt in the heat of the day. Now I gotta teach you how to keep ice frozen in the heat of the day. Come on. Vacation's over.'

I threw the water back into the pond and said while following Mr Jake, 'And he's back.'

Chapter 35

I TOOK MY DUTY AS the element even more seriously since the day I came to know about Mike's fate.

It's been a month since Mr Jake told me about the whole Mike-Ivy thing. He'd been looking more cheerful with each passing day. Sometimes, letting your feelings out feels good.

My family life was going as usual. But I was learning new techniques every week from Mr Jake.

Now I could freeze water, turn water into vapour, keep it in that state for as long as I wanted to, create a water hurricane, and other such stuff. And it was really fun.

This one day, we had the big Sunrise Valley Fair.

There were huge duties at the shop that day, unlike the other days.

I left for my job early in the morning. Jose, Mr Roy, Mr Jake, and a couple of other guys were unloading vegetable and grocery boxes from the truck. I joined in and helped them.

Then Mr Roy divided our duties. I was to pack things for the customers and make sure they got everything they paid for and also to write about them in the register and add up the total sum at the end of the day.

Didn't seem much of a tough job to me. Jose was to stay near the food counters and make sure nobody used foul methods of slipping food into their bags. And I was pretty sure that nobody would do something like that. Sunrise is a very small place.

Then as soon as the clock struck nine, the fair started. People flocked into shops like bees. Our shop wasn't much crowded, since who'd buy vegetables from a fair? But it was more crowded than other days.

I kept packing up the stuff that people gathered in their baskets and putting them into paper bags.

Jose went out of my view. And Mr Roy kept on urging me to work faster. Trust me, I was working faster than usual. But he should've cut me some slack. This was the first time that I was doing something like that.

Then around twelve, the crowd receded, and Mr Roy closed the shop for fifteen minutes. Outside, it was still crowded. Jose and I went to the garage and saw that Mr Jake was busy working on a new car.

'Come on, Uncle J., have something to eat,' pleaded Jose.

Without even looking up, Mr Jake said, 'Hun, I gotta fix this car. Then I'll eat.'

Another customer arrived, and he got busy talking with him.

So Jose and I went outside in the fair. We bought two burgers.

Jose said, 'So any news from you-know-who?'

'I don't know Voldemort personally,' I replied.

She laughed and said, 'I just have this stupid belief that if I name her, she'd show up here suddenly.'

'Nah. I haven't seen her lately. I'm missing her a lot, if you ask me,' I said, and we both laughed.

'So how's it going between you and Sam?' I asked, trying to change the subject.

'It's going great,' she said, blushing.

'I've seen that. He doesn't like leaving you alone a lot.'

She looked at me and said, 'Look, you can hang out with us any time you want to, Lin.'

'Yeah, right,' I said.

I guess my sarcasm wasn't evident enough in my words because she said, 'That'd be great!'

As if on cue, Sam showed up.

'Speaking of the devil,' I murmured.

I guess Jose heard me because she looked at Sam and said, 'Can we, like, hang out later? I wanna hang out with Lin right now.'

A secret understanding passed between them, and Sam said, 'Uh, sure. I just came to say hi. That's all. So see ya later, Lin, Jo.'

I looked at Jose, and she said, 'What? I wanna spend some time with my buddy.' And taking my hand, she said, 'Let's go to that shop.'

Chapter 36

IT WAS SUNDAY. REALLY sunny and cheerful. The birds were twittering. The bright blue sky was dotted with white fleecy clouds. But the day wasn't hot; it was kind of comfortable since a cool (yet dusty) breeze was blowing.

I'd gone to the shop at the right time. Jose was speaking to her dad. Mr Roy looked pretty agitated, which proved that she was telling him about her relationship with Sam.

I didn't want to interfere, so I went into the garage instead. But I saw that it was locked from the outside. Where was Mr Jake?

I had no other choice but to go to the shop.

Mr Roy was yelling at her. Oh god, why me? When I entered the shop, Mr Roy's voice calmed down. I guess he didn't like screaming in front of other people. I took a quick look at Jose and saw that she had tears in her eyes.

I went as far away from the counter as possible and started rearranging the already-arranged vegetables on the shelves.

'We'll talk about it later,' said Mr Roy in a harsh voice and stormed out of the shop.

I tried to look as busy as I could. Jose came up to me. I looked at her and said, 'Hey.'

She broke down into a fit of crying. Why me, again?

I tried to calm her down. When she was able to talk again, I asked, 'What happened?'

'Sam and I went to his grandma's house yesterday, which is a three-hour drive from here. I didn't tell my dad about it since I knew he wouldn't let me go. I thought I'd return before he notices. But we got stuck due to the storm last night, and I returned today morning. My dad's mad at me.'

'It's gonna be fine,' I said even though I thought that she should've at least called him. 'He's gonna come around. He's just trying to be dad-ly.'

She chuckled and said, 'What?'

'You know, all overprotective and stuff. It's gonna be fine.'

'You think so?'

'I know so.'

Then work started. It was a Sunday, so we had extra work. It was really crowded that day too, and each time people bought something, I summed up the cost with all the others before. I'd even been given a new job—to put whatever people buy into the paper bags for them to take home and also maintain things at the counter whenever Mr Roy wasn't around. Weird, how he trusted me more than Jose. Still, Jose had been kind of busy lately with Sam.

It was around eleven when Lucas came into the shop with a few other seniors. Amber was there too. On seeing me, he went, 'What're you doing here?'

'I got a job here,' I replied, wondering what he and his friends might have to do with vegetables and fruits. 'What're *you* doing here?' I asked as I packed up another paper bag with some potatoes and onions for a customer.

Lucas's friends were looking at the vegetables. He looked at his friends momentarily and said, 'We're going camping to this place. It's just an hour's drive. So we're buying stuff to cook there.'

I didn't have any more customers. Mr Roy had gone somewhere, so I was pretty sure that he wouldn't yell at me. Jose was sobbing in the storage room, I guess.

'Cool,' I said. 'You told Mom and Dad?'

'They won't even notice,' he said.

'That's kinda right,' I said, chuckling. His friends came over with some vegetables and fruits. I started packing them into a paper bag.

'That's your sister?' this brown-haired dude asked my brother.

Lucas nodded. 'Why doncha invite her to come with us?' the dude asked, grinning at me.

'She's too young for ya, man. And she's my sister, so stay away from her,' replied Lucas. I grew as red as tomato. Why was a senior interested in me?

'You guys go on out. I'm coming with the stuff,' said Lucas. When they'd left, he said, 'So how much do I owe you?'

'Seventeen dollars,' I replied.

As he took out the money and placed it on the counter, he said, 'Don't say yes if that guy asks you out,' pointing out at the door.

'Mr Why-Doncha-Invite-Her-Over?' I asked.

'Yep,' he said, shoving his wallet back into his pocket.

'Got it.'

Chapter 37

I T WAS ALMOST NOON when Mr Jake entered the shop with Mr Roy.

But the weird thing was, Mr Jake looked agitated, even more than Mr Roy. They were having a heated discussion. When Mr Roy stepped into the shop, he said something to Mr Jake that I could clearly hear: 'Keep my daughter outta this.'

This got me wondering what he might be talking about. When Mr Jake went into the garage, I excused myself and followed him there.

'What was that all about?' I asked when I entered the garage.

Mr Jake looked up at me from the little piece of paper that he was reading and said, 'W-what?'

'I asked what that was all about, with Mr Roy.'

'Oh, it's just—' He held out the paper to me and said, 'Take a look at this. I found this today on my car seat.'

I took the paper and saw what was written on it:

I think you and your little element girl wouldn't be foolish enough to let twenty children, or even more of them, die. And I know they would die if she doesn't cause a hindrance. Chemistry class tomorrow would be just so fun to watch.

~Ivy

'What the hell is wrong with her?' I asked with disgust in my face.

'I don't know,' replied Mr Jake.

'And whatever did she mean by the whole "Chemistry class tomorrow would be just so fun to watch" thing?'

'I don't know that either.'

'What *do* you know?' I asked, getting restless.

'That twenty children are going to die tomorrow,' he said, as casually as he'd say 'hi' to his friend.

Was he serious?

'And you're just gonna sit back and do nothing?' I spread out my hands in front of me in a 'what the hell' motion.

'Let me check my to-do list . . . Yep.'

I cursed him and said, 'Twenty children are going to die. Twenty children. Unless she's lying. And I don't find her to be the lying type.'

'She's not the lying type, especially not in these matters,' he said and started going through some papers on the wooden table at one corner of the garage.

'You can't do that. You have some responsibility.'

'Towards whom?' Saying this, he turned around.

It took me some time to think about the answer. Finally, I said, 'Towards those children.'

'Why?'

'Because you're their teacher,' I said after thinking momentarily.

He seemed to think about it and said, 'I think this is a trap.'

'And I think you just said that she's not the lying type,' I said, frowning at him.

'Oh, she isn't lying about the "twenty children dying" thing. I think it's a trap to get *you* to her. And that would be *bad* for you.'

'And tomorrow's chemistry class would be worse for those twenty children. Just tell me what I am supposed to do.'

He looked up at me from the papers and said, 'Nothing.'

My mouth hung open. 'Did you just say "nothing"?' I asked.

'Yeah.'

'Are you drunk?'

'I don't drink.'

'No. I mean, with stupidity.'

'I'm busy.' Saying this, he got a call (and I think it was a fake one), and he went out of the garage.

Oh, he was drunk alright, and not just with stupidity.

Chapter 38

THAT EVENING WHEN I returned home, I saw that there was nobody there. When I entered the kitchen, I found this note on the kitchen counter:

> Hey honey. Your dad and I got invited to his friend's house for this little get-together. I think there's food in the fridge. If not, there's money in the fruit basket. Buy something for yourself and Lucas.
>   P.S.—Lucy's with me. You don't have to worry about that.
>
>   ~Love, Mom.

Wow. I was surprised that she even remembered to write a note. Anyways, I didn't eat anything. I just changed my clothes and lay on my bed, thinking the matter over in my head. When I looked at the clock, it was already past nine.

And it was just about time for me to carry out my plan.

I put on an all-black outfit. I took out my black bag and put in stuff that I might need, like flashlights, extra batteries, pepper spray, and the like. And not to forget, my Aqua.

Then I set out on my errand.

When I reached the school building after transporting myself with the help of my powers, I rushed towards the school door. And then, just as I was about to touch the door handle, I realized something: it must be locked.

I started thinking what to do. It was almost ten thirty. I could use the water from the basins of the school washroom to open the door, but I'd not yet learned that trick well enough. Still I tried. It took a lot for me to even track the water since it was far away.

I felt the water better as it was coming towards me. Just as I was about to put it into the lock, I heard something, and the light in a room on the third floor was turned on.

I lost all my control over the water. Was it the watchman?

Still, I *had* to get in. I took control of the water and put it in the lock and realized something: the door wasn't locked.

'Stupid me,' I muttered as I turned the handle. 'All this work for nothing.'

I ran to the third floor. Just as I reached the room, I saw that it was the chemistry lab. Was it Ivy who turned on the light? But she might've wanted to creep up to me in the dark.

I slowly turned the door handle and saw who it was.

Chapter 39

It was Mr Jake.

'What're you doing here?' I asked with my eyes wide open.

'I must ask the same question to you,' he said, looking quite astonished himself. He was holding a test tube containing a pink liquid in his right hand, and a clipboard in the left one. There were other papers spread in front of him.

'Uh . . . I came here to save the lives of twenty children. What 'bout you?' I asked, putting my hands on my hips.

'Oh, I'm here for the same reason. But you shouldn't be here. I asked you to do nothing.' He put the papers down on the table.

'And I was supposed to listen to you?'

'Yes.'

'I'm sorry, but I couldn't risk the lives of twenty children.'

'I'm your teacher. You must trust me.'

'You also almost got me killed.'

'Once.'

Before I could answer, we heard something. I looked out into the hall. Mr Jake looked out the window.

'We must work fast. That might be the night guard or, worse, Ivy,' he said, putting the test tube on a test-tube holder and taking up a few more papers.

'What're you trying to do, anyways?' I asked, going over to the table.

'As far as I think, she put some explosive chemical in place of another not-so-explosive one. I'm just trying to figure that out.'

'Okay, so what're we looking for?'

'A green-coloured liquid, probably. It's Ivy's saliva. The saliva's really, really destructive. It acts as an acid, an explosive, a stain remover, and the like.'

'Never heard of something like that,' I murmured.

Mr Jake mixed the pink liquid with a blue one and said, 'That's because it's a unique one. Only Ivy can secrete it.'

Suddenly, we heard a loud bang. I started looking at the chemicals kept in beakers and test tubes on the shelves and said, 'Okay. Green liquid.'

To tell the truth, I was scared. I didn't feel ready enough to face Acid Lady. And I was pretty sure that getting burned with acid wouldn't be fun.

I found a light-green liquid kept on the fourth shelf and said, 'Got it!'

Mr Jake came running over, only to find that it was another one. I started looking for it again. Mr Jake suddenly said, 'Ivy won't be dumb enough to keep a green liquid in its real colour.'

'You mean, she might've changed the colour of the liquid?' I asked, turning around.

'I don't know. She might.'

And couldn't you have told me that a little earlier?

I started hearing a buzzing sound. Then it started growing louder. Mr Jake's back was turned towards the window. I looked at it, and whatever I saw froze my blood.

Chapter 40

'M R JAKE! BEHIND YOU!' I screamed.

It took a lot for me to come out of the shock.

I saw something rising outside the window—a black apparition. Then when the light from the room fell on her face, I realized who it was: Acid Lady.

'Go! Go go go!' screamed Mr Jake.

There was a weird thing about Ivy: she felt even more powerful. She was outside the glass window; still I could smell the stink.

I darted out the door, and Mr Jake followed me.

'What's the plan?' I screamed over the noise.

I guess I forgot to mention this: we could clearly hear a buzzing noise now. It was probably being made by Acid Lady's wings since there wasn't anybody else.

We ran past the Physics lab, and Mr Jake screamed, 'Right now, the plan is to run!'

I know that looking behind while running from the same thing isn't good, but I just *had* to look. What I saw made me trip and fall on the hallway. Acid Lady was floating in the air, behind us, her green hair floating too, and her eyes were bright green. Her wings seemed to be a blur. Everything else was the same. And I could smell her stink from the very end of the hallway.

Mr Jake helped me up, and we ran towards the one-way stairs to go upstairs to the terrace. But guess what? The stairs had wet cement on them. There was a sign in front of it saying 'WARNING!'

'What're we supposed to do now?' I asked.

Acid Lady was only, like, twenty feet away from me. She was advancing slowly now since she'd got us trapped.

Mr Jake looked about and said, 'Come here.'

He ran towards the hallway that leads to the English class. I followed his heels. We entered the room, and Mr Jake shut the door behind us. He went to the desk and started ruffling through some papers in the dark. I could see that he was extremely tensed.

'What're you doing?' I asked.

He didn't hear my question. Instead, he kept on muttering, 'Come on, come on, come on!'

Then we started hearing the buzzing sound real loudly again.

Without saying anything, Mr Jake took my wrist, and after peeking out the door, he ran towards the bathroom. I saw that there was something in his hand too.

When he shoved me into the men's room and entered it himself, he said, 'I know you can do this. I want you to transport yourself back to your bathroom, safe at your home. Get away from here, as far away as possible. Okay?'

'A-and what about you?' I asked, breathing loudly.

He showed me his left hand. There was something like a taser in his hand. 'I'll be fine.'

'A taser? A taser is nothing against her!' I screamed. The buzzing sound was getting louder.

'She doesn't want me. She wants you. Go!' he screamed over the noise.

'No! I can't leave you here!' The noise was louder.

'You have to!'

The door flew open, and in came Acid Lady, floating.

But I got a glance at Mr Jake's face momentarily, and I knew he wanted me to leave. And I would leave for him.

So I transported myself through the taps in the bathroom.

The last thing I remember seeing was Mr Jake pointing the taser at Acid Lady and a blinding bright light.

Chapter 41

When I opened my eyes again, what (or who) I saw shocked me. 'Lucas?' I screamed. I saw that the main door of the school was open.

Six people—four guys, two girls—were trying to open a locker. My brother was one of them. And then I realized where the banging noise was coming from: they were trying to break open the door. I'd been transported there through the water fountain.

Lucas turned around with eyes wide open and said, 'Lin?'

'What're you doing here?' we both asked each other simultaneously.

'Wow,' Amber exclaimed, 'that's what you call unison.'

There wasn't much light there, but I could see that all the kids, including my brother, looked drunk.

I looked at Lucas with a questioning glance. He did the same at me.

'You go first!' we both screamed again simultaneously. 'No, you!' This time, we'd both pointed our index fingers at each other.

'I saw you first!' I said.

Lucas couldn't argue. And then I realized something.

'Please don't tell me that you're doing something awful,' I said.

This brunette girl said, 'If nobody's gonna know who's doing this, it won't harm us, right?'

Now let me tell you what they were doing: they were putting water on everybody's things in their lockers. Stupid popular-kids stuff.

Then I remembered something: Acid Lady. I *had* to get my brother and his friends out of danger.

'Get outta here!' I screamed at them.

Amber rolled her eyes and said, 'Yeah, we will, after our work is finished.'

'You're not finishing your illegal work,' I said, tugging at my brother and the other girl. 'You guys, get outta here. It's not safe.'

'We love risks, sista,' another dude said.

'Don't ya "sista" me. Get out of here!'

And right then I heard the buzzing noise again. 'You guys hear that?' my brother asked.

'Oh no.' I was hyperventilating. The noise was coming from the hallway which leads to the main door.

I grabbed the main door handle and tried to turn it, but I knew it was Acid Lady's magic which prevented me from opening it.

I grabbed Lucas's hand and shouted at the others, 'Follow me!'

It was a good thing that they did what I asked them to. I shoved them into the principal's room and said, 'Stay here. Don't come out, okay?'

Before I went back out into the hallway, Lucas said, 'Where're you going?'

Instead of answering him, I shut the door and put a water chain on the lock. Mr Jake had taught me how to do that.

I ran towards the stairs. The sound was growing louder as I advanced towards the stairs. Just as I was about to put my feet on the first step, guess who floated slowly down the stairs?

None other than Acid Lady.

I started backing up, my hands ready to defend myself with my powers at all times.

'Where's Mr Jake?' I asked with shaky breath. Acid Lady descended on the fifth step and said with that same hissing voice, 'Where do you think he is, sweetheart?'

'I asked where Mr Jake is!' I screamed. I had to keep her away from Lucas and his friends.

I mean, seriously? He had to bring his friends here *that* day?

'Don't be so aggressive!' she screamed at me. 'The less aggressive you are, the longer you will live. But you will have to die at one point, like your Mr Jake did.'

'You're lying!' I screamed. She'd already descended three steps.

I wouldn't care if she'd kill me (actually, I guess I would). But I had my brother and his friends to save too. And I wanted to see for myself whether Mr Jake had actually died or not.

'Oh no, I'm not, honey,' she said, descending another step. I think I should mention this—with every step that she was descending, I was backing up.

'You're evil. You hurt Mr Jake. And you also killed Mike.' Anything to keep her from killing Lucas and his friends.

She paused for a moment and said, 'You're wrong. It was your Mr Jake who hurt me. He left me when he saw this form of mine.'

'Any guy would,' I said. Uh-oh.

In her green eyes, I could see a green flame. She started floating again, jumped from the stairs, and attacked me. I was ready enough for this. I rolled to my left and attacked her by surrounding her with water from the washroom (I managed to add some toilet water too). Then I folded my fists and froze the water.

This gave me enough time to get up and dart towards the corridor on my left, which led to the gymnasium.

Chapter 42

FREEZING THE WATER AROUND Acid Lady just bought me enough time to get up and run. But I wasn't even a feet away from her when she broke the ice and floated behind me.

I increased my speed. I opened the gymnasium door and formed a water chain on the door handle. Acid Lady kept on pushing the door, but the door didn't fly open for some time.

This bought me enough time to run towards the gym's locker room. The locker room had water taps and showers in it, which would help me.

I'd just reached the shower and hid myself in one corner when I started hearing the buzzing noise again.

I could feel the smell getting stronger as Acid Lady floated through the chambers and melted the plastic seats.

'Where are you, element girl?' her voice hissed.

I momentarily stopped breathing for fear that she'd hear me. The buzzing sound receded. When I believed that she'd left the locker room, I slowly got up. I didn't know what to do. I was confused, scared, lonely, and had lives to save.

Yeah, right, Mom, I am *real* lazy.

I listened to the quietness for some time. When I decided that everything was safe, I fully got up and stepped out of the shower room. But someone had kept their towel on the hanger outside the shower room, and it brushed against my hand and fell down. I thought that Acid Lady won't be able to hear the light thud of a towel falling on the floor, but before I even knew it, the buzzing sound was speeding towards me.

I did the only thing I could: I went into the shower room again, turned on a shower, and transported myself to the water fountain (that was the first thing that came into my mind).

This time, I saw Lucas tiptoeing out of the principal's room (how'd he break the water chain, I'd like to know).

Lucas was startled on seeing me, and I said, 'Shh.'

I tiptoed towards him and whispered, 'What're you doing out here? Go back where I left you.'

'How'd you arrive here?' he asked with wide eyes. Apparently, he'd seen me coming out of the water fountain.

'No time to explain,' I said hurriedly.

Then I took his hand and started tiptoeing towards the principal's room, trying to get him to safety.

'You should've stayed where I left you,' I whispered.

'Well,' he whispered, 'for one, you left so mysteriously.' We were nearing the principal's room.

'It was all only for your good.'

'Seriously, what's going on?'

'I'll tell ya later.'

'Why later? Why not now? And why are we whispering?'

Right then in front of us, Acid Lady descended from the roof. It felt like she came through the floor of the first floor and down the ceiling of the ground floor.

'Well, well,' she hissed, while floating down to the floor, 'you've brought acquaintance.'

I looked at Lucas, and trust me, in my whole fifteen years of life, I'd never seen him as frightened and confused as he was right then. He looked both shocked and disgusted.

'What do you want, Acid Lady?' I asked, getting frustrated.

'Well, for now, I want you to stop calling me Acid Lady. That's a filthy name.'

Yeah, like you, I added in my mind.

'I'm done with games. It's all over now, Linda.'

As soon as she spelled my name, I attacked her, and she attacked me too. I could see something blue, like glowing water, coming out of my palms as I spread them in front of me. Lucas kept on looking at us with disbelief.

'What're you looking at? Run!' I screamed even though I could feel Acid Lady's power growing stronger.

Lucas, instead of running towards the principal's office, ran into the room which was the nearest.

Acid Lady won. She put an extra-powerful thrust at the end, which threw me a couple of feet across the hall. She floated towards me. Suddenly, I couldn't feel any air reaching my lungs.

I grasped my neck and gasped for air.

Then I felt an invisible tug on my neck. Somebody was pulling me up while choking me. It was Acid Lady, of course. She was advancing slowly towards me. I was pulled up until my feet stopped touching the floor.

I felt the green eyes of hers disappearing from my view. I'd have given anything back then to just stare into those horrible eyes of hers.

I felt the whole world disappearing from my view. I still gasped for air. I stopped tugging at those invisible hands on my neck.

Slowly, my hands fell down, lifeless.

My eyes could no longer stay open. My eyelids slowly started growing heavy. I could feel the sweat on my forehead.

I still kept on gasping for air, but my energy decreased.

Suddenly, everything started growing into a sphere, which became smaller and smaller with each passing second.

The last thing I remember seeing was a stick-like figure come out of a room in the hallway.

Then the sphere closed into a tiny dot.

Chapter 43

I COULD BREATHE AGAIN!

As I fell down with a thud to the floor, I touched my neck and took in long, deep breaths. I coughed a few times. I could breathe again. Only someone in my situation—and I hope none falls in such a situation ever—can understand how blessed I felt right then.

I looked at Acid Lady and that stick figure. Apparently, the stick figure was of my brother's. He was running down the hallway, throwing *buckets* at Acid Lady, as she chased him.

I had to admire his guts, though.

Without wasting any more time, I rushed down the hallway. I attacked Acid Lady with my hot-water trick, and as soon as the ball of boiling water touched her back, she turned around and started chasing me.

'We are not playing tag!' she screamed.

'Oh, we are,' screamed Lucas and threw a couple more of small blue buckets at her. This made her turn on him.

I again attacked her, but this time with my frozen-water trick, which I'd applied before too. I guess I was just too distracted before to control it. This time, I got to say this, I nailed it!

Acid Lady froze in the middle of the hallway. I covered every inch of her body and clothing with ice.

I screamed at Lucas, 'Come on! This'll buy us just a couple more minutes. We gotta hurry.'

He threw the buckets on the floor and, running with me, said, 'Woohoo! That was fun!'

Yeah, right, fun if you're just throwing buckets at a super-dangerous creature. So *not* fun if your life actually depends on how well you defend yourself from that creature.

We ran to the gymnasium. I remembered something that I'd seen there that'd help me.

I shoved Lucas into the basketball court and said, 'Wait here.'

I went up to the main switchboard, called him there, and described my plan to him as fast as I could. He did as I asked him to.

Then I went back to the place where I'd frozen Acid Lady. She was still frozen as I'd left her. I was almost fifteen feet away from her when I broke the spell. As soon as she was freed, she darted towards me.

I waited for her to come near enough as to see where I was.

'Oh, you're going down!' she hissed angrily.

'Let's see who's going down,' I said and ran into the gym. I was ten feet away from the door when she broke in, floating off the ground.

She attacked, and I counteracted it. She attacked again, and this time, I rolled to my right. As soon as I was up, I attacked her. I surrounded her with water, but this time, I didn't freeze it.

Even if she attacked me, with the water surrounding her, I didn't let go. I held the water around her tightly. Then I screamed, 'Now!'

Two thick wires, one red and one blue, were dropped from the catwalk on the ceiling by Lucas, which electrified the water and electrocuted Acid Lady.

For a moment, I could see green and white sparks. Then an explosion occurred, which made me close my eyes and guard them with my hands. I could feel a few places of my skin burn, like on my arms and stuff.

When I opened my eyes, they filled with tears.

Chapter 44

I saw nothing—just a little bit of fire, the burnt wooden floor, smoke, and dust. The scoreboard had dropped to the floor, and it was burning too, throwing sparks and stuff. Lucas came down from the catwalk, and we hugged each other.

Then pulling away, I said, 'Why did you drop the whole scoreboard? We can't pay for that thing.'

'It just dropped. Wasn't my fault. And that thing's, like, antique. They needed to change it,' he replied, laughing at the last part.

'And you just helped them do that.' I laughed too.

Then I turned towards the mess and said, 'There's a fire extinguisher in the locker room. We better put it out.'

'You can do that, right?' he said, looking at me with a questioning glance.

I rolled my eyes and said, 'It'll freak you out.'

'Try me.'

I pointed at the fire, and a gush of water swept towards it from the locker room and extinguished the fire.

'Wow, well, that was freaky,' Lucas said with eyes wide open, shaking his head. 'So I don't think your favourite teacher, Mr Jake, would be happy about you destroying the basketball court.'

And then I remembered: Mr Jake!

I rushed out of the court with Lucas running after me. He screamed, 'Where're you going?' But I was too distracted and tensed to answer him.

All kinds of thoughts were going around in my head. What if he died? No, he couldn't die. I mean, he had a taser. Tasers always keep you safe, right? But the chances of him living were next to nothing.

I climbed all three flights of stairs without waiting for any breath. When I reached the washroom, what I saw made me gasp. Mr Jake was lying on the floor, the taser lying a foot away from him. He was lying on his back, all soaked in water, his hands and legs spread, like a star.

I knelt beside him. Lucas just rushed in, and seeing Mr Jake lying motionless, he came towards his lifeless body slowly.

'Mr Jake?' I managed to choke out.

'Mr Jake?' I said again. When no answer or movement came, I sniffed. Lucas put his hand on my shoulder and knelt beside me.

Tears started streaming down my cheeks. Lucas hugged me, and I cried.

I managed to choke out again, 'Mr Jake?'

This time, I felt like his eyelashes moved. I tore away from Lucas and leaned over Mr Jake and said, 'Can you hear me?'

Lucas started saying, 'Lin, I think he's—'

But I stopped him and said, 'No! I saw his eyelashes move.'

'You did?' he said, looking shocked. He looked at Mr Jake, trying to notice any movement.

'Yeah, I did. Can you hear me, Mr Jake?' The last part I said to Mr Jake.

I saw his eyelashes move again. This time, Lucas saw it too. He leaned over Mr Jake too and felt his pulse.

'He's alive!' he exclaimed.

'We should call 911!' Saying this, I took out my phone. But it was wet due to the shower thing. I cursed.

'Where's your phone?' I asked Lucas.

'I left it in the truck, I guess,' he said, feeling his pockets.

'Go get it!'

'No, wait, I'm fine,' Mr Jake croaked in a really low voice.

'Mr Jake, can you hear me?' I asked, looking at him with wide eyes, gasping. Lucas too had knelt beside me after Mr Jake said that he was fine.

'Yeah, ye—' He started to get up. Then he coughed a good deal, throwing up some water too. When he was well enough to speak, I hugged him. Mr Jake hugged me too. Then Lucas also joined in the hug.

We'd been hugging for some time when Lucas said, 'It's getting weirder . . .'

Mr Jake let us go, and then he laughed heartily. This proved that he was all right.

'So what happened?' I asked.

'Well, when you transported yourself, you broke most of the plumbing in here because you brought in too much water pressure. We gotta work on that,' he replied.

Then we both laughed.

'This makes any sense to you guys? 'Cause it doesn't make any sense to me,' Lucas said with one of his eyebrows up.

I looked at Mr Jake, and a secret understanding passed between us. Then I turned to Lucas and, taking his hand, said, 'Let's go outside. Let us get refreshed, and then I'll tell you everything.'

Saying this, we all got up and went to search for the others.

Chapter 45

Lucas's friends were so drunk that they'd fallen asleep in the principal's room. We tried to wake them up, but they only murmured weird stuff in their sleep. This one guy said 'lemonades'.

So Mr Jake asked us not to wake them up. When Lucas asked whether they'd get into trouble, Mr Jake didn't say anything and went out into the hallway with a smug grin on his face.

Out in the hallway, water lay around here and there. We went out of the school.

It was almost dawn then. A few birds were twittering. The darkness of the night was disappearing.

'So is she gonna return?' I asked as we were just about to set foot on the highway.

'No. Once you kill a, um, dangerous creature, it doesn't return until after a few centuries.'

'So, like, I've kinda saved a few future elements from this stinky, ugly, dangerous creature?' I asked.

Mr Jake said, glaring at me, 'But there are other creatures too, just about as dangerous as Ivy. And the future elements need to tackle them.'

'Still not making any sense to me,' Lucas murmured.

'It will, buddy, it will when I tell you all about it,' I said.

After we reached home, I soaked in the hot tub for, like, an hour. As I soaked in there, I turned over all that had happened the previous night in my mind. Somehow, my head felt lighter. I felt happier and safer.

I was on the verge of giving it all up, risking life on earth. And if someone had asked me whether I wanted to give it up right at the moment when I was facing Acid Lady in the school hallway, I'd have said, 'Yeah, sure, buddy. All yours.'

But I was glad that I didn't give up. I got an amazing friend and an elemental-skills teacher. And I think this whole move thing brought me closer to my brother, if not my family.

At times, life feels like it'd given up on you. But never, ever give up on yourself.

Life is dynamic; it is always changing. It has its ups and downs. Sometimes change feels good. Like, change brought me closer to something magical and dangerous (and I'm referring to the Aqua and my elemental skills here, not Acid Lady). It also brought me to an amazing and friendly place. And I'm still glad that I didn't give up so easily. Because change brings challenges. And it's just better if you face those challenges instead of avoiding them or hiding from them, because at one time, they're going to catch up with you. Some changes might be good; some might be bad.

But what it all comes down to is this: it's on *you* to decide whether to make the best or worst out of those changes.

Chapter 46

IT WAS ALMOST SEVEN in the morning as I paced the kitchen, while Lucas sat at the table along with Mr Jake. They'd both freshened up just like me.

'So, like, are you planning on telling me the truth or . . . ?' asked Lucas.

'Well, if you don't wanna know, I don't wanna feed it to you,' I replied, seeing hope flicker to get out of this mess.

'Um, so I decide to stay and hear ya out.'

I made my sad-puppy face and looked at Mr Jake, who was munching hungrily on dry cereal. He didn't notice me at first, but when he did, he looked up at me and said, 'Don't look at me. It's on you to decide. He's *your* brother, not mine.'

'Seriously?' I said, spreading out my hands in front of me. 'I don't think I can take it any more, all this pressure.' Saying this, I went over and sat at the table.

'Which is good. You can tell me all about it. This'll help reduce the pressure on you. Right?' Saying this, Lucas looked at Mr Jake hopefully.

'Yeah, the boy's right. Or else we might have another major tap problem,' replied Mr Jake. And as he cracked the joke, he laughed, and Lucas joined in too without even understanding anything.

I groaned and said, 'Okay, fine, here goes.'

And then I went ahead and told him all about the necklace, Aqua; the first water element, Aqua, and the other elements; and how I got the powers. Then I described to him my encounters with Acid Lady (and each time I said 'Acid Lady', Mr Jake corrected it with 'Ivy'). Then I finally told him about how she wanted to put the lives of children in danger. Right then it hit me.

'What if she didn't lie?' I asked Mr Jake, suddenly startled at my own realization.

'What?' he asked, still chewing on dry cereals (how could he eat those things?).

'What if Acid Lady—'

'Ivy.'

'Ivy, whatever. What if she wasn't lying about risking the lives of children? What if the thing which is gonna hurt them is still there?'

'Well, as she's dead—and if she wasn't lying—her saliva won't even function. It dies with its producer. And if she was lying, then it'd save us a great deal of hassle.'

'What do you mean?'

'Well, people would be curious about the unidentified substance—'

'Does it hurt to say UFO?' murmured Lucas.

Mr Jake ignored his comment and continued, 'Specially your chemistry teacher, Mr Mondi. He's always curious about everything.'

Then he got up, dusted his hands of the cereal dust, and said, 'Well, let me go and check on it, whether we're clear of suspicion or not.'

'You make it sound like a crime, whereas Lin was just trying to save lives,' Lucas said.

Mr Jake laughed and said, 'Well, I'll leave now. See ya later, Lin, Lucas. And you're still having that job, Lin, so don't miss out on shifts. We'll cut cash from your salary.'

'Oh, give me a break!' I groaned yet laughing.

He left, leaving me with Lucas.

'So you didn't trust me enough to tell me about such a huge thing in your life?' asked Lucas, turning towards me.

I ask you, how're you supposed to answer a question like that? But I didn't want to lie to him any more, so I said, 'Look, it's just . . .

we never actually talked before, you know. We weren't like brothers and sisters. We're more like strangers back then.'

'So you didn't trust me?' He made me sound guilty.

'Of course, I didn't. I'm sorry, you're a great brother. And there are many things in my life that I don't tell you.'

'Why not?' He shrugged.

'Because I thought you wouldn't understand!'

'What?' He frowned.

'Well, you're the popular kid. Popular kids don't understand most stuff. I've had my experience, you know.'

'But you're my sister. I'm always here for you. You can talk to me. And I'll try to understand as much as I can.'

'Well, do you understand this, this whole element thing?'

'I said I'll understand understandable things.'

'You did not!' I laughed. He laughed too.

And I realized that I was wrong to judge him. It was the lack of hanging out together that made me not trust my brother enough. But actually, he's a great brother, one with whom you can fight yet share your deepest secrets. Well, at least only secrets.

'I promise: no more secrets from you. Well, no more secrets-that-I-can-tell-you from you.'

'I promise the same. So can I share a secret with you?' he said, leaning in.

'Yeah, sure.'

'I don't like Amber,' he whispered, as if he was telling me something of grave importance.

'Like that wasn't evident enough!'

And we both burst out laughing. Right then our doorbell rang. We both rushed to open the door. It was Mom and Dad along with Lucy and Tess.

'Hi,' Mom said. 'Thought you guys wouldn't be up yet.'

I laughed and said, taking Lucy from her, 'We're up early.'

'For the first time,' added Dad while he was taking off his shoes.

'You guys returned so early too,' I said.

'Oh, we were worried sick about you. It's a new place, you know,' replied Mom. Huh. They were worried sick about us. This was a first too.

Mom gave me a box and said, 'Doughnuts for all.'

Lucy started screaming, 'Doughnuts! Doughnuts!'

I laughed and said, 'You're gonna get them!'

And for the first time, our family *felt* like a family.

'So what did you guys do last night?' asked Dad.

I looked at Lucas, and he looked back at me. Then we both grinned and said, 'Just the usual stuff, you know.'

Chapter 47

IT WAS A MONDAY, so there was school. We got dressed up real fast and took the bus to school.

It looked like Mr Jake had cleared up most of the mess. There wasn't any water lying in the hallways. And most of the stuff that we'd dropped or Acid Lady had destroyed were pretty much back to their original selves.

The only sign of the fight was the fallen scoreboard and tons of water in the basketball court. Guess he overlooked that.

But the coach was claiming it as an accident since the board was really old. The water, on the other hand, couldn't be explained.

School was pretty much the same. Jose didn't ask me a lot of questions about the fight. But she did ask me quite a good deal of them.

Mr Jake couldn't be seen at the school that day.

My necklace, Aqua, had started glowing with a bright hue of blue, which meant that I'd stored a lot of power in it.

When I went to the shop after school and entered the garage, there were two people too many in there.

There was an old guy, probably the same age as Mr Jake.

He had brunette hair, light hazel eyes, and a soothing smile on his face, with wrinkles by his eyes. This gave him the appearance of

Santa Claus since he looked kind of heavy. He looked a bit Mexican. He was wearing a light-blue shirt with khaki trousers that looked a million years old and flip-flops. All of his clothes seemed charred. I know what Mandy would've said if she'd seen him: major wardrobe malfunction.

And standing beside him was the hottest guy that I'd ever seen. He had a unique eye colour: golden. Not brown. Not hazel. But golden. His eyes gave him a unique appearance. He seemed older than me, but not much.

His face wasn't happy. He looked pretty bored by the chit-chat of the old guys. And there were cuts and scratches on his face, with a big cut on his lower lip, which was bleeding. There was dust accumulated on his face too, as if he'd journeyed for a long time and got no time to wash up.

He was pretty tall, probably six feet, with dark blonde hair. He looked a bit tanned. He had that Greek God thing going on—broad shoulders and muscular build, you know. I could see it clean through his burnt orange shirt (now, what was up with that?). With that, he was wearing a pair of jeans, which looked charred at places. And he had black sneakers on.

Mr Jake was having an important discussion with the guy of his age, and the younger guy was just looking here and there.

I cleared my throat, and Mr Jake looked up. Then he waved at me to come in and said, putting his hand on the old guy's shoulder, 'This here is Diego, my old friend. He was also the previous fire element.'

He held out his hand, and I shook it. 'Hi, nice to meet you,' I said, smiling.

'I guess this young lady is the water element, Linda?' Diego asked.

'Oh, yes, she is,' replied Mr Jake.

The hot guy looked interested.

'I heard how you defeated Ivy,' said Diego.

I nodded.

Diego pointed at the hot guy and said, 'Meet Josh.'

I turned towards him with a smile, but I got lost in his golden eyes. He shook my hand that I'd held out to him. His hands were pretty rough and a bit grimy, and his grip was firm, like a person with strength, and not just physical strength, but also intelligence. He smiled too, and oh, those dimples were to *die for*. He said, 'Hi.'

This got me back to reality, and I said, 'Hello.'
Diego said, 'Josh is the fire element.'
And that explained his burnt outfit.
And the orange erect-triangle necklace he was wearing.

About the Author

Poulami Ghosh is a ninth-grade student and was born in the Indian city of Kolkata in West Bengal. She was brought up by her working parents and lives with them. Her father is an engineer in a private firm, and her mother is a government employee. Writing has always been her passion. She has even got a few articles published in a newspaper for schoolkids, called *TTIS*. Her first book, *My Little Trip to Georginia*, was published on 8 March 2013. Undoubtedly, her second book, *The Elements: Water*, would also be appreciated by the teenage readership for which she is writing.